Mike Thomas-Hall grew up in Wales in the Rhondda Valley, but he never met Rhondda. Just as well because in Sydney, Australia, he met Belinda and she was an answer to a prayer. Four sons and 50 years later, they are still very grateful for each other. They live in the lush hills of the Tweed Valley in New South Wales, and you are very welcome to drop in.

I would like to dedicate this book to the author of inspiration and to all the helpers along the way: Belinda, Alex, Denise, Kevin, Pam, the bitumen guy, Jesse, Pete, Skye, James and my mum, Wendy.

Michael Peter Thomas-Hall

A MERE SHEPHERD BOY

Book 1: The Youngest Son

AUSTIN MACAULEY PUBLISHERS™
LONDON • CAMBRIDGE • NEW YORK • SHARJAH

A CIP catalogue record for this title is available from the British Library.

ISBN 9781398489004 (Paperback)
ISBN 9781398489011 (Hardback)
ISBN 9781398489028 (ePub e-book)

www.austinmacauley.co.uk

First Published 2024
Austin Macauley Publishers Ltd®
1 Canada Square
Canary Wharf
London
E14 5AA

I would like in particular to acknowledge the dauntless Cunningham Geikie, whose book *The Holy Land and the Bible* was written during his travels through that land in the 1880s. Reading his account is like going there. He saw it and he described it—in intricate detail. To see it as he saw it is no longer possible, but to see it through his eyes is to see the land as it was in Bible times. As a companion volume to the Bible itself, his book, together with the illustrations made by his co-traveller H. A. Harper, is a portal into the past.

Table of Contents

Chapter 1
In Bethlehem

Shalom.

Shalom… That means: "Peace, harmony, wholeness… peace be with you… lovely to see you… hello… farewell… may God's face shine upon you…" It has a special feeling to it, the word 'Shalom'. It makes me want to raise my hands and dance. It rings with the bells of antiquity.

Well… my story begins… deep in the mists of antiquity. Long before I was born. Before time began, in fact. I was always a living glimmer in the heart of God, along with yourself, and those around you… So – who am I? Let me give you a clue – but don't jump to conclusions. I was born in Bethlehem, and my father's name began with 'J'. No… no: not Him. He appeared many generations later, and if my life is significant (which it is), there are no words in Heaven or Earth able to describe His. Except, maybe – 'Wonderful' and 'Marvellous'… but really, even those words fall well short. I wish my life was marvellous and wonderful; and in some places it was, but… there were other places… many other places… where I fell short. I tried to model myself on Him, whom I had never seen, and sometimes I got close, I think. It was a good feeling when that happened.

So – who am I? You may have worked it out already, but I'll try to remain anonymous for a little longer. There is a very famous statue of me somewhere in the world. Very famous indeed, but it was done more than two thousand years after my life had concluded – so how did the sculptor know I looked like that? It is indeed a very beautiful statue, classical, and even breath-taking. But is that what I looked like? I won't say right now. Hopefully, you will build up a picture of me as we move on through my life.

Regarding that beautiful sculpture: if I ever did come to look like that, in the beginning I looked nothing like it. I was a new-born, just like everyone else. But I wasn't a firstborn; I was actually last. Lucky last. I had seven brothers and two big sisters. We lived in a small cluster of stone huts and everyone in the village knew each other. As soon as I could walk, my sisters made sure I helped with the housework. One of the chores was collecting dried animal dung; we used it for fuel. That was a never-ending job. Goat dung was my favourite. It came out in little pebbles, and after a day or two was just right for playing marbles, or throwing, or hitting with a stick.

Collecting water was too heavy for me when I was little, and anyway, it was woman's work. But I liked to go to the well at the end of the day with my sisters, because all the world was there, meeting and talking and drawing water. The sunsets were often beautiful, and I would get lost in wonder – until Zeruiah poked me with her foot to let me know we were going. She was my older sister. Much older. By the time I was ten she had three sons of her own. Zeruiah was a powerhouse, full of determination, blue-eyed and robust. Very unusual. My father depended on her in so many ways. She was a champion water carrier. Other women could only carry half her load. And so handsome! She worked in the fields harder than any man. There was something magical about her and about her name. Zer-oo-i-ah. Zeruiah. When you say it right, it sounds like a breath of wind sweeping over wild places. There are many wild places where we live. I love to watch her brushing her hair in the firelight after our evening meal and listen to her sing and watch her dance. She married an alien, or so she told me. Trust her – she was a law unto herself. His name… was… well, I'm not sure. But his grave is in Bethlehem. I never saw him.

Anyway, back to the housework. Turning figs was another job. The figs were placed on drying racks and later pressed into cakes. We had to preserve figs and olives and wheat and barley. And meat and cheese and yoghurt and lentils and honey. Also, almonds and forest fruits and nuts. We were always busy. I loved the sound of the bees in the almond blossoms in early spring. How busy they were!

As I grew up, I learnt about the history of our tribe and our rules and customs. Each week we had a day off when there was no work and… no play. On this particular day, we learnt about our history and the events and the people who had come before. I was just a little boy in an obscure hill village: a village like many others.

"My son," my father impressed upon me. "Our history is a rich heritage, given to us by God. It is the most precious thing we possess."

I wasn't too sure about that. I really fancied one of those slings the shepherd boys were always practicing with. I thought that one of them would be even more precious. All my brothers had slings. I borrowed one once and didn't let go at the exact right moment – and cracked myself in the head with a rock. It was embarrassing, but I decided I would get really, really good at it – just to prove to myself I could. I would practise.

My father explained how important it was to obey our rules. Work hard. Honour God. Be clean. Be obedient. If we followed these rules, we would be able to live a life free from the hardships of war and disease and famine. It sounded good to me and I was a keen student. But inside – I was longing for the day when I could go off and look after the sheep all by myself – and admire the wildness and the beauty of the hills, and sing songs to God, and lead the flocks into green pastures and beside still waters.

There was that other aspect to our lives, however. Why were my father and older brothers often seen gazing into the distance with furrowed brows and clenched jaws? What were they hoping not to see? And what were those night-time fires doing springing up on the hilltops from year to year, and where did my two oldest brothers go with their slings and their swords, and would they come back? Sometimes they were away for months, and every week my father, Jesse, would pack up provisions onto a donkey and send a trusted servant to deliver it. Figs, raisins, cheese, flour, wine. The only thing they didn't need was water. This, being so vital, they found a way to provide for themselves. Every man in the army had his own water-skin made out of goat-hide. Naturally, they had spears and swords and arrows as well, though these were a recent improvement. In bygone years there was not a blacksmith in our land; we had been under the heel of our enemies then, and they kept us without weapons.

So – who were the enemy, you might be wondering? We had lots of enemies. Lots and lots. Over every inland hill and down by the great blue sea, which I had heard of but only seen shimmering in the distance. Enemies. Many of them were historic enemies. Once upon a time they had been related to us, but now, generations later, they served different gods and they lived in other lands… but they weren't far away. A two-day walk could bring you into the land of Moab. As a matter of interest, my great grandmother, Ruth, came from Moab. She was a Moabitess. This doesn't mean she used to bite people. Far from it. Her story was, in fact, a great inspiration to me. My father related the story to us many times. It goes like this:

Naomi of Bethlehem, our ancestor, went with her husband and their two sons to the land of Moab to escape a terrible famine. They lived there and both her sons married Moabite women. One of these women was Ruth, the other was Orpah.

Alas! Naomi's husband and two sons both died – and the three women became widows. Broken-hearted and bitter, Naomi made up her mind to return to Bethlehem. She told her two daughters-in-law to leave her and return to their own people. Orpah said goodbye but Ruth refused to go. Despite Naomi's protests, she accompanied her mother-in-law. She wanted to look after her, and to worship our God.

They made the journey back to Bethlehem and one day a generous and Godly man – Boaz, my great grandfather – allowed Ruth to glean in his cornfields. He was so impressed with her diligence and her faithfulness to her mother-in-law, that he asked Naomi for permission to marry her. I liked how he told his reapers to make sure they spilt some extra wheat for her. Whenever I glean in the harvest fields, I spill a little for the other gleaners, and I always think of Ruth, and it makes me want to be faithful and diligent and to serve God with a humble heart, just like she did. I told Eliab this one day, and he laughed at me. Eliab: he's so big and handsome and full of himself – my oldest brother. Oh well, let him think what he thinks. As for me… I will keep on thinking this way.

So, what am I up to? Housework, enemies, my family… did I tell you the name of our tribe? We belong to the tribe of Judah. Judah was one of our ancestors; he was a son of Jacob. Our tribe were shepherds and itinerant farmers, and for centuries our predecessors roamed the lands with their flocks and herds. It was a dangerous life, what with other hostile tribes and nations – and drought, and famine, and disease. But somehow, we survived. We became slaves in Egypt for four hundred years, and then amazingly, we all walked out. Our God organised the whole thing. He's the reason our tiny nation survives, but it's still a precarious existence.

Some of our people live in fear of our enemies, but I feel perfectly secure. I believe I could kill lions and bears and giants with my bare hands… if God wanted me to. So does Abishai, my nephew. He is Zeruiah's oldest son: one year younger than me, and a powerhouse. I have seen him grab a charging goat by the horns and throw him over his shoulder – and he is only ten! He's been to the crags and come back with a baby eagle to prove it. The crags is the place where you get to see the sea from. The highest crags, I mean. The only thing Abishai fears is Zeruiah, his mother. She's got two other boys, Joab and Asahel. We are growing up together. I'm the leader, of course. I am older and wiser, and kinder. And more Godly. At least I think I am. They really look up to me and are always trying to impress me, especially Joab. There is something about that kid though, which I am just not comfortable with. I'd much prefer him to be my friend than my enemy, however. At least I know that much. We wrestle, we race… we play war games. We practice with our slings.

Jared the tanner taught us how to make the slings. We helped him to scrape some hides. We spy out on other villages. Life is amazing. There are other boys who like to come with us. One day we will all be soldiers. Everyone has to be. It's the only way to survive, so we might as well start early. We believe that God will look after us, but not if we aren't prepared to look after ourselves.

I have a teacher – one of the elders of the village. Ishpah, his name is. Michael, my little friend, always sneezes when he sees me talking to him, trying to make me laugh. Ishpah is so serious, so passionate, and yet still a little bit humorous. He wears a linen robe with a camel hair waistcoat. He is bearded, of course; all the men are, except in times of deep mourning, and he has flashing dark eyes and a black turban. I don't know what it's made of. Wild bear, Michael reckons, but it's probably just goat. How do the women make all these different types of cloth, I wonder? Sheep, flax, goat, camel. It's amazing what they can make into cloth, but they get plenty of practice, that's for sure. Abigail, my other married sister, and Zeruiah and my mother, are busy from dawn to dusk. If it's not spinning cloth, it's preparing food, or harvesting or planting, and they take pride in it. I've been told that there are some women who only ever make cloth, and they even spin it out of gold. This is for the king and the chief priests and the commanders of the army. We never see anything like that in Bethlehem. But we do have craftsmen here as well, in metal and wood and leather, and we pay for what we need with goods or with silver. We don't see much gold; at least I don't – except for earrings and nose-rings and other jewellery – but that's only on special occasions.

Special occasions. They come around every now and again; several times a year I'm told. But what's a year? It seems more like an eternity. On these occasions we might get visited by strangers in rich robes, who read us our laws and customs, and we treat them like royalty. Maybe they are royalty. Then the offerings and celebrations begin and can last for a few days, or a week. Animals are offered on an altar because that is part of the law which God gave us, as an atonement for our sins. Bullocks, goats, lambs, even pigeons: without shedding of blood there is no atonement. Everything is done according to the law, or at least it's supposed to be. These are very solemn occasions. Some offerings are completely consumed with fire, the rest are divided among the people and eaten.

Wedding feasts are another special occasion, and these are lavish affairs with food and wine and dancing. They often last for a week. I wonder how long mine will last? Only a day or two, I suppose, since I am likely to be just another poor shepherd boy. Anyway, back to my teacher – Ishpah. His favourite story is the story of Joseph, and we have heard him tell that story many times. It's my favourite story too. I'll tell you why, and I haven't told anyone else this. It's because I feel like Joseph myself: specially chosen by God. The youngest son with lots of brothers – who have no time for him. A dreamer. I'm always dreaming, but I dream when I'm awake. Joseph was asleep when he dreamed. He dreamed of being lifted up into high places of power and authority by God, and his dreams sustained him through his dark years when he was betrayed, enslaved, and imprisoned. I wonder if I'll have any dark years? Joseph always held his head high and behaved uprightly, and humbly, and faithfully. That's what I want to be like too, and I believe that even if I am only a shepherd in the hills, or a soldier for King Saul, I can still be like Joseph in my heart and God will be pleased with me. What could be more important?

THE COUNTRY AROUND BETHLEHEM

Chapter 2
Blind Man's Buff

Well, one day we were having a game of blind man's buff on the edge of the forest. We were in a little flat-bottomed ravine with a stream running through it. It was our special playground. We knew fifty different ways to get out of this ravine and we could evacuate the place in different directions in seconds. So, when danger threatened – like a lion or a bear, or a leopard or a wolf – or Eliab, my big, bossy, grown-up brother – or our enemies from other lands – we could flee like rabbits. Especially Asahel. He could run like a deer, and yet he was only six: five years my junior. He was the youngest and most favoured of the Bethlehem boys. I was the oldest and the leader. Abishai and Joab, my nephews, were my faithful deputies. They were like young lions. I had to treat them with kid gloves one minute, and steely eyes the next. It was the only way to preserve unity in our ranks. Strong leadership was the key. To anyone watching, we were just a typical bunch of village kids making the most of our time away from chores, but in our own eyes we were heroes – dauntless warriors – fearless fighters.

I had my own special rock, which overlooked the ravine, sheltered by an ancient olive tree. It was a wild olive, and the fruit it bore were small and bitter, not like the grafted trees that grew in the fields. But we boiled up the olives with water and wild honey and had a warriors' feast. Our pot was a copper helmet brought back from a raid by Abinadab, my brother – my father's second son. He gave it to me.

So – Blind Man's Buff. Our version of this game was not for the faint-hearted or the weak. The blind man had his eyes bound with a length of linen cloth several times around, to render him completely sightless. This precious cloth served us faithfully, and we treasured it. We washed it, we dried it, we stored it in a dry place. One of the boys' mothers gave it to us. It came from Beth Ashbea, the linen town. Washing was part of normal life for us; clothes, hands, bodies. It was something our tribe did, washing and sacrificing and keeping clean. It was part of our law. We boys all wore similar clothes: a linen under-tunic and a rough, outer cloak, usually dark blue or brown, since we were peasants. The outer cloak didn't need to get washed much since it wasn't worn all the time. Long and loose, with loose sleeves, it was an all-weather protection system. We often slept in it, usually on a bed of sheepskins, with tussocks of dead grass underneath.

My bed was always so springy and comfortable: I made sure it was. What sensual dreams I had as I grew up! Where did they come from, I wondered? Sometimes I watched the women drawing water from the village well in the early morning and was smitten by their grace and beauty. The younger ones, that is. They were unveiled: our women only wore veils at special times. But rarely would they meet my eyes.

"What are you doing, you little troublemaker?" Eliab demanded sourly one morning, catching me watching at the well. He was already married with children of his own and was on his way to pasture his flock. What could I say? Zeruiah raised her head from drawing water and flashed me a look. She knew what I was doing there, even if I didn't myself. The look melted into a brief smile and she returned to her work. Strengthened by my sister's smile, I sprang out of my brother's way and trotted off to do my work, which in this case was turning the flax stalks on our roof while the dry weather was still holding.

Holding was something the dry weather did quite well in this land of ours. Water was precious, and it fell seasonally. For ten months of the year the sun shone brilliantly. Our labour was to preserve and to store, to plough and to sow, to shepherd and to husband. We were an industrious people, and the land we had inherited from our fathers, mere generations ago, was described as a land flowing with milk and honey. And who was it that described it in this way? None other than our very own God: The Lord.

All the nations around us had their own gods. These gods varied quite a lot and there were lots of them, but we only had one. And the other nations also had their own kings – and had done so for many generations. We had only just got our first king – a few years ago – and this was not what our God wanted, but… He permitted it. Saul was his name: our first king, that is. That's who my brothers were fighting for, and one day – my turn would come.

Milk and honey. When I was little, I wondered if I might see the rivers of milk and honey flowing through our land.

Where were they to be found, and how sticky would they be? I liked milk and honey. Goat's milk, cow's milk, sheep's milk, camel's milk. Once I made the mistake of asking my father if we could drink mule's milk. The whole family was sitting outside around a cheerful fire on the hard-packed earth, next to Zeruiah's simple stone home. It was a cool, starry, autumn evening; the sort of evening when tales are told, history is recounted and little ones fall asleep snuggled up in the warmth of the fire and family. The village was dotted with similar family groups. Only the watchers at the gate and in the tower were absent. A lull occurred in the conversation and I took my chance. "Father," I enquired respectfully, "I love goat's milk best, but I do love cow's milk, and sheep and even camel, but is it possible for us to have mule's milk?"

An astonished silence greeted this enquiry, followed by an outbreak of mirth and merriment. That was quite embarrassing. Even the little children were laughing freely – without knowing why, of course. My father smiled at me and was about to reply, when Eliab leant forward with a mocking expression: "You," he uttered, loudly and deliberately, commanding the attention of the whole group: "… are a little donkey!"

Redoubled mirth and merriment broke out at this sally. I had no idea why. I stared at Eliab speechlessly. My face turned red. I felt as if the top of my head was glowing with heat. My father reached out a strong old arm and drew me to his side. I willed myself not to resist him, but to come under his authority and love. He drew me close. The roughness of his cloak tingled against the fire in my cheek. I could smell the strong, clean smell of our countryside clinging to him, like a soothing perfume. I was four years old, and I still didn't know what I had said that was silly. My pride was hurt. But… but… I was nestled into the strong warmth and protective embrace of my father, like a shy chick peering through its mother's feathers. I watched my way through the rest of that memorable evening.

I was still wide awake when we began to retire to bed, and felt puzzled, but restored. Eliab came over and placed his hands on his forehead and inclined his head towards me. It was his way of showing that he was sorry for his offence. I gazed at him mutely. He would never know how valuable this little act of brotherly repentance was to me. For him the event was quickly forgotten. Not so for me. But that night I fell asleep as soon as I touched the sheepskins – and dreamed invincible dreams. I dreamed of being strong and resolute, faithful and brave, sheltered beneath the arm of the Almighty. I was just drifting into the golden glow of Heaven on a cloud of heavenly music that uplifted my spirit and bore me up like an eagle – when familiar voices called me back from my ecstasy, and I discovered I was in my own home – and another day in Bethlehem was about to begin.

Anyway – back once more to the boyhood game which I was describing before this digression began: back… to the Blind Man's Buff.

"Asahel! Asahel!"

From my rocky throne in our valley, I called out who was to be the first competitor in our game: little Asahel – the six-year-old – whose brothers were Abishai and Joab. Zeruiah's sons. They watched over him like hawks. The linen band was wound around his head. Now, he was the blind man. Next would come three warning claps – followed by the buff, which was a blow to the chest. Joel was his first assailant. He took his stand before Asahel and the other kids clapped in unison three times.

Clap! Clap! Clap! Buff!

The blow to his chest sent Asahel sprawling, but he leapt up gamely.

"Who hit you? Who hit you?" the boys chorused.

"It was Ethan," he squeaked.

"No, no! Withdraw – or stand again!" came the chorus.

At this point the blind man could withdraw… or he could stand again. Had he guessed correctly, then Joel would have become the next blind man. If Asahel decided to withdraw, then I – the leader – would choose the next competitor. But… the little one decided to go for glory. He would stand again. Going for glory was the enticement that lured our boyish hearts. We wanted to stand tall and proud before the onslaught of our fellows – to resist the temptation to withdraw – to break through the pain barrier… This surely was to become a man among men, a hero, a great one.

The undisputed champion in our ranks was Abishai, who could withstand the kick of a mule, or so it seemed. Often, he would not even name his assailant, but shrugging off the blow would call out that fateful word – "Again!" And here was little Asahel, emulating his brother and calling out:

"Again!"

Amasa, my sister Abigail's son, stepped forward. As he did so, Joab placed a restraining hand on his shoulder, as if to say – 'Go easy on my little brother'. Amasa glanced at him cockily – and took his place in front of the blind man.

Clap! Clap! Clap! Buff!

Amasa unleashed a blow that flattened his cousin. We looked on with horror. Would he recover? The faces of Joab and Abishai were a dread to behold: their precious little brother, Asahel – smashed to the ground like a broken pot. Amazingly, the little fellow rolled over and crouched on all fours, gasping like a stranded fish. He was still alive.

"Who hit you, who hit you?" came the chorus.

"Amasa!" he screamed.

Shouts of excitement greeted this pronouncement, and Ethan and Joel sat Asahel down on a fallen tree and unwound the cloth from his eyes with unusual care and sensitivity. Joab and Abishai skulked in the background, looking on with black brows, eating berries.

Now that the blind man had identified his attacker, it was the attacker's turn to be the next blind man, and it was Asahel's privilege to choose the first assailant. I had a sense of foreboding about what might happen next – and so did Amasa. He looked apprehensive and vulnerable, as the linen cloth covered his eyes. I could sense a test of leadership coming.

"Mighty God. God of Heaven and Earth," I intoned: "See me through this challenge."

Amasa stood, waiting for the buff. He was a strongly made boy, ten years old, the same age as Abishai. He was a good, solid member of our boy-tribe, easy to get on with, friendly, brave, willing – but sometimes cocky and stupid: and today was one of those days. I was comfortable being around Amasa, which is more than I could say about the sons of Zeruiah – but could I depend upon him as I knew I could depend upon them? Even as these thoughts ran through my mind, the two brothers approached the blindfolded Amasa. Which one would it be? Abishai or Joab?

Joab, of course. He would get his way. He always did. He stood before the hapless Amasa, a dangerous light in his dark eyes, while Abishai looked on.

Clap! Clap! Buff! Clap!

Unexpectedly and underhandedly, Joab struck between the second and third clap. He struck with the smoothness and precision of a panther. He caught his unprepared cousin below the ribs, and laid him to the ground, winded and unable to breathe, and fighting for air.

"Who hit you, who hit you?" came the chorus – but feebly – as the shock of this low act of betrayal sank in. There came no reply. Amasa was out of action, and it would be some time before he recovered. Ethan unwound him. The rest of the group turned around and looked to me on my rock. I greeted their shocked eyes with a merry look that came from I know not where, and nimbly leapt down into their midst.

"The next contestant," I proclaimed: "… will be – me! Ethan – you choose my assailant!"

This unexpected change of direction rallied the troops under my banner and brought a new focus to the moment. It also enabled Amasa to be no longer the centre of attention. He leant pale-faced against a tree for support, avoiding our eyes, recuperating; grateful to be out of the spotlight. Ceremoniously, my closed eyes were bandaged and all light faded away. Three times they turned me around and then I stood, exposed and anticipative, before my unknown assailant. I felt light of heart and untouchable, every sense highly tuned and vibrating. I smelt the scent of berries in front of me. Abishai. Just as I had expected. I knew his technique by heart: three claps, a two second delay and then the strike. I waited like a coiled spring.

Clap! Clap! Clap! At the moment of impact – buff! – I swayed backwards – and allowed the force of the blow to bowl me over in a graceful reverse somersault, regaining my feet in one smooth motion. Cries of admiration broke out from my companions.

"Who hit you, who hit you?" they chorused.

I waited for a suspenseful second then: "Asahel!" I exclaimed. More cries broke out, this time of laughter.

"No, no!" they responded. "Stand again!"

"I will not!" I decreed, shaking off the linen cloth, and tossing my chestnut hair. "I withdraw."

Darts of admiration shot out at me from every eye, most especially those of Joab and Abishai. I held each heart in my hand. It felt good to be loved and worshiped: how different were these companions from my brothers at home. I could see that Amasa had recovered some composure and I pulled him to his feet in a comradely gesture then ran swiftly to the head of the ravine. The rest followed me by diverse ways and we returned to our homes, battered, but carefree and intact.

*

"That was a low act!" little Michael declared when I spoke with him early the next day. The sun was just coming over the horizon behind us as we walked, making our shadows long. "Why did you not rebuke him? Why did you not rebuke Joab and punish him? Why do you always let him get his own way? You are the leader!"

I wriggled uncomfortably. Yesterday was gone; I didn't want it brought back.

"Look, it's over now. It served Amasa right. You saw what he did to Asahel. He shouldn't have been so rough – and so stupid."

"Yes, but he didn't cheat, did he? Joab cheated. He hit him before the time – and he hit him too low!"

I shrugged: "What can I do? What can anyone do? The sons of Zeruiah are a law unto themselves."

"The sons of Zeruiah," Michael echoed scornfully: "Pah!" He spat on the ground: "That's what I think of the sons of Zeruiah!"

A long shadow fell on us from behind, and I placed a cautionary hand on his shoulder: "Joab is behind us," I hissed.

Michael paled, and a hunted expression twisted his sweet, boyish face. He glanced quickly behind him and gasped in relief when he saw it was actually one of my brothers who was walking towards us, and not the dreaded Joab. I poked him in the chest merrily, enjoying his discomfiture, and gave him a brotherly hug.

"I have to go. Don't think any more about it, it's behind us."

I left my little friend speechless and fell into step with my brother, Shammah. Today I was helping him with the sheep.

Chapter 3
A Princess and a Harp

"Integrity. That's the key word. Integrity. That's how God wants us to live our lives. We trust in God and walk in integrity. Do you understand?"

Ishpah looked at me with piercing eyes. He was sitting on a low stool; I was at his feet.

"Of course I understand!" I responded confidently. "You've told me many times before."

"But are you?" he demanded. "Are you walking in integrity?"

"Well, as much as I can. I'm only a boy, don't forget."

"David. Do you want to please the Lord?"

"Yes Rabbi, you know I do."

"Yes, I know you do. I just wonder sometimes. Tell me," he added, quietly: "Where did you get that pouch from?"

"My sling pouch? I swapped it with Michael. We're friends."

"I know you are friends. Isn't that all the more reason why you should treat him like a friend?"

"But I do!" I defended myself.

"That pouch is far superior to the one you gave him. Yours was old and cracked. This one is soft and new. It wasn't a fair swap."

"Look, Michael wanted me to have it because I'm the leader. It's only right that I should have a good sling pouch. And I'm the best! It's only right."

My persistent teacher interrupted: "It's only right that you conduct yourself with integrity. And this, I think, is something you have not done. I may be wrong, but I think you have used your position to get something that you wanted – in an unrighteous way." He paused and waited. He did not have to wait long. I took the pouch and belt off my waist and placed it on the ground between us.

"I have sinned," I confessed. "It is as you say."

"You are fortunate," Ishpah told me gently, "… because you can undo this evil. You can undo it. It is not always the case. Show me your reading now."

He pointed to one of several slim, clay tiles that were impressed with written characters. I picked it up and began to read.

"The Lord God, compassionate and gracious, slow to anger, who forgives iniquity and sin, yet will by no means leave the guilty unpunished, visiting the iniquity of the fathers on the children and grandchildren, to the third and fourth generations."

"You don't deal treacherously with God," Ishpah interrupted dryly, "nor with your brother who trusts you. God is to be feared. You are reading it well, but doing it well is what matters. Do you know what happened to King Saul?"

My interest was immediately aroused. "No. What happened?"

"This happened not so long ago, only a year or two, in the war against the Amalekites. King Saul was specifically instructed to take no prisoners and to take no plunder. Samuel brought him this message – from God. But he took their king as a prisoner – and kept back the best of the herds. This was direct disobedience – and it was not his first offence. Because of this, the Lord took away his Holy Spirit from Saul, and will choose another man to replace him. The Lord will choose another king."

"Really? Who will he choose? How do you know?"

My teacher gazed at me solemnly. "I know this because the prophet Samuel told me. Samuel trusts me... and – David... I trust you. I have told no one else, and I want you to tell no one."

"I understand. I will be faithful to your trust. You can rely on my integrity in this matter."

"That is why I told you. It is a test for you: a test of integrity. The Lord looks into every part of a man's heart. He searches the hearts of men. He is looking into your heart. Will he be pleased with what he sees?"

"I hope so."

"I hope so too. Now – I want you to copy this passage out on a square of goat's skin. Very finely, mind. Use soot with a little oil and pay great attention to the spacing. Use a fine quill and seal the finished work, then roll it up and place it among your treasures. And *look* at it from time to time – and remember, God looks on the heart. You have to keep your heart pure. This is the meaning of integrity. And I want you to learn the passage by heart. This passage is for you. Learn it, live by it, always remember it. Be blessed, my son."

"Thank-you, my teacher."

I looked at Ishpah. Was I dismissed? It was hard to tell. My teacher was looking off into the middle distance, drifting off. He did this sometimes and I had learnt to be patient. In fact, I rather enjoyed these times and made the most of my own thoughts. I waited.

*

Today was the Sabbath morning. A day dedicated to the Lord, when no work was to be done. It was hard work, doing nothing. I gazed over the flat roofs of the village to the hills beyond. As the hills grew higher, they became barer, and in the distance black and grey dots moved slowly over the brown pastures. Goats and sheep. The rains were long gone and there was little green to be seen in the hills, apart from the ribbons of trees that wound up the gullies and dotted the pastures. Beyond and below the forests laid a hold on the land. Oaks and acacias spread ancient branches over the busy byways that led to other habitations. The wheat harvest was being brought in and the grapes were forming on the vine. Soon the autumn winds would sweep through our houses and the pace of life would change. It would be the time for storing and preparing and repairing. Also, a time for fixing roofs, and lining grain silos, and storing wine, and drying raisins and dates. Dates were a luxury in Bethlehem. Date palms grew, but they produced little fruit. Most of our dates came with the desert traders from Sinai and from Jericho and were bartered for with grain and goats.

These desert traders were dark-skinned and white-turbaned. They travelled in large caravans with camels and donkeys and were ever on the move. If I knew their language what tales they could have told me… what cities, what paths, what places they must have been to. Here am I, a little village boy, learning about sheep and flax and barley, and collecting dung. And here are they, travellers to the far corners of the Earth, bringing all kinds of wonderful, unimaginable treasures: silk, spices, incense, gold, silver, musical instruments, clothing, weapons, dates… And such secretive and mysterious people! The women veiled, the children hidden behind skirts, the men alert and impassive.

There were two treasures they brought that I particularly coveted, apart from the dates. And one of these treasures was free, but you had to be quick to get it: camel dung. It was so dry you could burn it as soon as it hit the ground! We watched the camp with eager, boyish eyes, and were quick to take what we could from the edges of the circle. But the nomads were jealous of what was theirs. They had as much need of fuel as we did. So, after some years I reasoned that an easier and even fairer way of obtaining this exotic commodity, camel dung: was to barter. But what did we poor village boys have to barter with? The obvious answer was goat dung and sticks. There was no shortage of sticks in the deep forest. The edges were pretty much cleared, so it was a long walk and a big job. Our fathers approved of the idea, however. Trade was trade: they encouraged our business acumen. So, year by year we laid in stores of sticks, gathered by hand and carried on our backs – and we traded.

When I was ten, I waited one morning near the nomads' camp with Abishai and Joab. They were like two eager, dark ferrets at my shoulder. Some little nomad boys approached us with shy smiles. In the background, hawk-like eyes watched over our transaction. We did the trade: our bag was full of camel dung and the boys returned to their camp with bundles of sticks. As we turned to go, a sweet melodic sound caused us to turn around. Where was that music coming from? A nomad stood at a tent entrance. His hawk-like eyes met mine with a flash, and his hand pointed down. It was a summons. I glanced sidelong at Abishai and Joab.

"I'm going in. Watch out for me."

"They'll drink your blood!" Joab warned darkly. Abishai grinned.

I walked inside the camp. As I did so, a strange feeling came over me. I was walking into forbidden territory. Unseen eyes were watching me. I might never get out. I might be taken away like Joseph to be sold as a slave in Egypt. What was I doing? The hand of fear that began to close over my heart made my knees weaken, but I remembered God; I remembered to believe in his protection, and my eyes brightened. I came before the face of the man who had beckoned me. He touched his hand to his chest as a token of friendship. "Shalom," I murmured with a little bow.

The eyes seemed less hawk-like – almost gentle. He gestured towards the tent, inviting me to go in. There was still time to run.

I stepped into the tent.

It was a goats-hair tent, dark brown in colour, but the morning sun came through the gaps and lit up the interior. Dust specks danced in the sunrays. Sitting on an ancient rug was a woman sewing. Next to her was a young girl who turned inquisitive eyes towards me. Those eyes reminded me of a deer, looking up from the dew: soulful, dreamy, beautiful, timid. I imagined the face behind the veil and was enraptured.

The girl turned away, stealing the faintest glance at me, and that glance stole my heart. I would gladly be sold as a slave for her, I thought. Her father spoke a few words in quiet, soothing accents, and the girl leant forwards and started choosing articles of sale for me to look at.

There were bangles and beads, ebony and ivory, sandalwood and cinnamon, gold and silver, copper and alabaster. It was like a miniature feast of treasure, but where were the bows, the arrows, the sling-shots and the shields? Where were the important things of life? The girl picked out a small concave mirror, made of polished silver or tin. She angled it so that both our reflections could be seen, and there we were, captured in this other world. I noticed with a shock how fair my skin seemed against hers, and how different our hair and eyes were. She was a beauty from the desert with raven locks and dark, all-seeing eyes. I was chestnut-haired and ruddy. The sunrays caused golden flashes of light to bounce off our glossy tresses. I looked into the eyes in the mirror before me and the eyes in the mirror looked back. It was only a moment, but it stays with me still. A woman: the most beautiful of all God's creations.

The soft voice behind us spoke again, and the girl picked up a pipe and blew over it gently, producing a breathless little note that hardly carried beyond the tent, but it carried to the ears of a baby goat that was curled, unseen, in the deep tent folds. The little creature stretched and shook and padded over and nuzzled into my beloved's side. She drew it close and stroked it for a moment. I felt envious of the attention, absurd boy that I was. I wished I was that goat.

In our home in Bethlehem, we often kept a lamb or a baby goat. They made charming pets and soon became everyone's favourite, nosing their way into every comfortable corner and forbidden place. After rainy spells we would pasture them on the rooftop, where fine grass sprang up for a season. We give our pets names, in fact, every sheep in a flock has its own name. They recognise their names – and the voice of their shepherd. This I find quite marvellous, since in every other way sheep are amazingly stupid: eating the wrong things, going astray, getting stuck on rock ledges… Not like goats. Goats are survivors. But I must admit, I have a soft spot for sheep.

The girl laid down the pipe and reached for a short, bone-handled knife that glinted in the sun. I drew in my breath, suddenly aware of my vulnerable position. These were Ishmaelites: the same people who had carried Joseph away to slavery. What was I doing here? I felt the presence of the man behind me and remembered Joab's dire prediction: "They'll drink your blood."

At that particular moment a cloud, probably the only one in the sky, chose to obscure the sun for a few seconds, and the tent became dark and gloomy. My imagination raced. But, the seconds passed, the light returned, and the soft voice, kind and reassuring, spoke again. At last, the young girl reached out for the one item that my heart was yearning for. The harp: the instrument that had called me here in the first place. It was made of dark acacia wood, rubbed with wax, and had eleven strings; five thick and six thin, each with a tuning peg that fitted into the curved arch. The base was hollowed out to magnify the sound, and the instrument was a convenient size for carrying. I could imagine myself sitting under a tree in the solitary hills, overseeing my own flock and making heavenly music.

The girl turned to face me and plucked on the strings. Her fingers were fine and supple, and she played a delicate, quaint, repetitive melody on the top strings, underpinned by a slow, progressive refrain on the bottom ones. It made me think of the wind winnowing the chaff away as the grain was thrown skywards in harvest. A harvest song: and this was harvest time, which was why the nomads were here. They were trading for grain. There was no wheat or barley in the desert, and even if there was, these people never stayed in one place long enough to raise it. The nomad girl handed me the harp, or lyre as it would be more correctly called, since it was only small, and as she did so her downcast eyes softened into a smile and a tiny glance escaped in my direction.

She can read my mind, I thought, gladly yielding to the ongoing magic of these moments… she has placed the harp in my hands and I will play her a love song. A sweet, naïve, innocent, boyish love song – such as only these unskilled hands could play. I held the harp as she had and plucked and stroked the strings with reverence and with zeal. I imagined I was a leaf falling from a high tree into a mountain stream, floating down the waters to the deeps below. When the last notes died out there was silence in the tent. The woman had stopped sewing and was looking at me. The girl sat archly before me, like a princess. The man made no move or sound.

Gently, I replaced the harp in the hands of my mountain stream. Would this be the last we would see of each other? I stood up and as I did so the man leant forward and presented me with a small gift, as was customary with strangers. It was a wooden stylus used for impressing letters onto damp clay. I accepted the gift with appreciation. The man tapped the harp, then he stood before me with an empty travelling bag in his hands. It was made from a whole camel hide and separated into two compartments, so it could be slung over a living camel's back. It could hold almost a homer of grain, I reckoned: that's half a camel load. "Wheat," he said, very clearly in our language. A homer of wheat for a harp, in other words. I bowed and backed out of the tent, as if in the presence of royalty. A cool breeze wrapped around my ankles, and I bowed again before casting a keen glance towards the spot where I had left my trusty lieutenants. They were still there.

I speedily re-joined them and we returned post haste to our long day of farm chores that lay ahead. It would be a year before I saw the traders again. That was now over a year ago…

*

So… I sat at the feet of my teacher, wondering when my princess would come, with a far-away look in my eye… and it was now me who was in the land of dreams. Suddenly I became aware that Ishpah was studying me with an amused expression on his face.

"Aha!" said he, smiling: "Where have you been? Dreaming again? Was it Egypt, or the desert, or the wide blue sea?"

"It was the desert," I smiled frankly. "Or at least something to do with the desert." I fingered the wooden stylus – the gift.

"Ah, the beloved…" Ishpah murmured: "Will you see her again?"

"I hope so, indeed. It is well into harvest time and if the traders return, maybe I will see her. I am able to purchase the harp. All year I have worked extra hard and we are having a good harvest, God be praised – and my father will come with me with a homer of wheat to make the trade."

"A homer? For a harp? What about the homerless?"

"We look after the homeless, as you know, quite well – and our few slaves and servants are content and happy, even though poor. They would not leave us if we paid them! But my father is willing to do this for me. Not so my brothers, of course. They consider it a terrible waste and a very bad deal."

"Tut tut!" Ishpah smacked his lips together with a gentle chuckle: "David, David… a harp… for a shepherd boy… in only his eleventh harvest. Why not a coat of colours, to make their outrage complete? Well, I hope you'll learn how to play it, and not leave it out in the rain."

"As if I would!" I smiled: "I'll treat it with kid gloves. I'll oil it, I'll wax it, I'll wrap it. I'll treat it with care – and I will sing songs of praise to our God with it."

"Where?"

"Where? On the mountains, on the roof, in the gate, beside the well! I am dreaming of the day."

"Dreaming again, always dreaming. But it is a good thing – to dream."

"Yes, provided they are good dreams. And Ishpah, what are your dreams about? I noticed that it was you who first began to dream this morning."

"Was it indeed?" He regarded me quizzically: "And is it the place of the pupil to examine the teacher? Does the servant question the master?"

"No indeed, my teacher. Please forgive my curiosity."

"Your curiosity I can forgive," he responded wryly, "but what can be done about your impropriety?"

He looked at me with raised eye-brows. I coloured.

"However," he continued: "I will gratify your interest – and perhaps it is not so unseemly… My dreams… my dreams… my dreams are from of old. I dream of Moses, of Abraham, of Adam."

"What about Eve?"

"Why – you cheeky little colt! Am I to hand you over to your father for a sound thrashing, or shall I do it myself?" Ishpah stood up with his beard bristling in outrage.

I placed my hands humbly before my bowed head and strove to explain myself: "But… my dear teacher… Ishpah, my master… Always, always have I heard of Abraham, and of Moses and Jacob and Joshua, and I am blessed indeed – but just this once, can you not tell me about the mother of all? Often have I hungered to know of her. Can you not tell?"

"What can be told?" Ishpah muttered contemplatively, resuming his seat once more: "Very well – let me tell you what I dream of on this matter. (I nodded) So… the mother of all was created… fully grown and wondrously beautiful… more beautiful by far than we could imagine. She was how old, I wonder? Maybe seventeen harvests – maybe… And naked and unashamed, as was Adam. And did she not walk with Adam in the evenings in the garden with God? And did she not move like a living spirit through the garden beside her husband, in the time when the world was young? When there was no care, no despair, no shadow of grief or mourning, and… no death. Think of Eve in the garden, and all is of radiant beauty, of peace and tranquillity, of hope, of love, and of adventure."

"Of adventure?"

"But of course, my unimaginative little dreamer: the adventure of a mind fully open to appreciate all the facets of the limitless beauty and wonder of God's creation. From the far-flung heavens to the tiniest flower, from the scent of the forest to the touch of the earth, and, and… not just riding lions and sleeping amidst tigers, but communing with God himself, the author of the universe. And, you know of course, that Eve and her husband were not idle. No indeed. They tended the garden, they tended the animals. It was the work that Yahweh, our God, had given them to do. And yet – it was not work – it was their place in creation… to be the stewards of all that God had brought into being.

Can you not imagine her, our mother – so perfect, so beautiful, so unaware – and yet in such harmony with the Spirit of God? Our God – the Father of lights. I can just see the radiance of a thousand stars cascading down her hair and enfolding her body in a mantle of light. I can see the tiny star-shaped flowers opening wider and turning in unison at her approach. I can feel the calm thrill of life – pure life – perfect, God-breathed life – passing like a song through the new creation, and Her – walking hand in hand with Yahweh himself.

Now this is Eve in the Garden – when all was as God intended: a woman so perfect and so at one with God and with her husband, Adam – that not even a daisy would be bruised beneath her heel. A woman who carried the image of her Maker in all his glory, and who brought the presence of God into every moment and movement. Not only this," Ishpah added in a lower tone: "… but one day that same heel, which would not bruise the daisy, would bruise the Enemy of us all. The very enemy who deceived her and brought about all this earthly suffering that we experience. His head would be bruised beneath the heel of the seed of the woman. He would be overcome and defeated."

"When?"

"We are still waiting, but it will come. There. Enough dreams for today. Did you like my dream of Eve?"

"Yes indeed! Thank you for reaching into your imagination for me."

"You are welcome. Your interest is always welcome. May the Lord keep you my son – and make his face shine upon you."

"May he keep you too, my teacher."

"May it please him so to do."

I returned home thoughtfully. Wondering when I would see my desert princess.

The very next week, to my great joy, the traders returned – and I got my harp! Did I see my princess? I did not. But she was there, I knew. I could feel her eyes upon me.

Chapter 4
The Second Encounter

"Brothers! Today is the day when we will go out and come back… and defeat the Benjamin Bullies! Give me your hands, each of you."

The Bethlehem Boys looked at me, their fearless leader, with a steadfast spirit. As bidden, each one placed his hand on the worn stone around which we were gathered in our hidden valley. Twenty-one brown, boyish hands overlapped each other. There was Michael, my sweet and timid confidant, who would follow me to the ends of the Earth, if I let him. There was Ethan, Asahel, Joel, Ahi, Micah and Elkanah. There was Amasa, my sturdy little cousin. And, most reassuringly, there was Abishai and Joab: how strong and reassuring their youthful hands looked – like those of young soldiers. And why did they look like that? Because… they almost were… Soldiers, that is.

Some months had passed since our first encounter with the Benjamin Bullies, and now it was late autumn. The grape harvest was in and every single person, old and young, slave and free, had been working from dawn to dusk, preserving the fruits of our vineyards: it was the season for wine-making and for hanging up bunches of grapes to dry… and for sampling the fresh fruit. Now that the work was over, we had a day off. A whole day. In the previous months our fellowship had grown stronger. We were a force to be reckoned with – or so we thought.

I was still the lamp. The leader. But there had emerged from our ranks a lesser lamp, one around whom many of the boys clustered, like bees to a choice flower, and who inspired his followers to be courageous and loyal beyond what I had ever imagined. And who was this lesser lamp? And how did he attract and keep his ardent followers? It was Joab – none other – and he did it without trying; it came naturally. He was born to lead, born to inspire. He gave no favours, sang no praises, yielded no quarter; yet the loyalty he received was unbreakable. Even Abishai, his older brother, was his devoted lieutenant. And what a lieutenant to have! Strong, courageous, daring. They were like two lions: the pride of the pride. So how secure was my leadership? It was even more secure. Joab saw something in me – I don't know what it was – that he regarded as special; something he himself did not possess. Some divine spark of spirit elevated me in his eyes. As much as Abishai was his first lieutenant, so was he mine. So, there we were, the three of us, a God-breathed cord that could not easily be broken. And it was greatly to my advantage, since not only could Joab turn mere boys into heroes with his war games and his presence, but he also kept our followers at a distance from me and gave me space – and I liked space; I needed space.

I needed to meditate, to cast my eyes to the heavens, to look deep into the waters, to watch the women at the well. To puzzle over the chameleons and moles and observe things only to be seen in stillness. To worship God in my heart. I didn't want to be up to my elbows in adoring glances! It was too tiring and intrusive. It made me lose contact with my soul. But Joab had no such problems – an aura of personal power kept his adorers at a respectful distance, and the only moles and chameleons he saw were instantly targets for his homemade javelin, or a rock – and he was a good shot.

Well, before I describe our memorable second encounter with the Benjamin Bullies – I had better describe the first one. But first: a little background. Let me explain:

Our tribe – Judah, the lion – overlapped with another tribe – Benjamin, the wolf. Various frightening accounts of the prowess of the tribe of Benjamin had reached our ears through my warlike brothers. There were ten thousand men of Benjamin, each a fearless warrior, so they said, who could fire both bow and slingshot with left and right hand. These hardened, wolfish men (whom we had never set eyes on) assumed terrifying proportions in our boyish minds, and we were glad they were our brothers, not our enemies. Was not King Saul himself of the tribe of Benjamin? Abner, son of Ner – Saul's commander-in-chief – was also of Benjamin. Abner had a reputation as a leader and a man of war. The men under his leadership looked up to him in the same way that our little band looked up to Joab. Abner had been through countless campaigns against our enemies, experiencing both defeats and victories – and on every occasion had come through – battle-scarred, but intact. He was built like a bull, so my brother Abinadab declared, and was both tireless and wily. It was just as well that Saul had his cousin Abner to support him.

Whilst a courageous and worthy leader, chosen by God through the prophet Samuel, Saul was in dire need of Abner's military talents, just as I was of Joab's.

*

Well, back to the bullies. Before our memorable second encounter there was indeed a first – which was not so memorable, and which I will now recount. This is what happened the first time:

A few weeks after our memorable game of blind man's buff, we went on an expedition. There had been a big wedding: the whole town came to a standstill for a week, and when we saw our chance, we took it. Twenty boys headed into the mountains for the day, looking for adventure, taking what food and weapons we could.

Unbeknownst to us, a similar expedition was heading towards us from Benjamin: a group of hard-headed boys bent on mischief. They carried slings as we did, and no sooner had we come into view of each other than they yelled their tribal war cry, slung their rocks, and then raced towards us as if we were Philistines! Instinctively I looked for cover. "The rocks!" Joab shouted, leading a scramble up to the hilltop crags. Stones clattered behind us, both those thrown by the enemy and those our feet dislodged in the mad dash. We attained the crags and loaded our slings.

Joab stepped forward unbidden. "Come no further!" he ordered, and the advancing boys stopped and sized him up. They were a rough looking bunch, led by a shifty looking youth, skinny and lean. I took my position next to Joab and spoke with more confidence than I felt.

"Weapons or no weapons?" I challenged them.

"As the Lord lives," the lean boy uttered, adding a foul word or two in a blood-chilling tone: "It matters not to me."

"Throw down your weapons then, and advance!" I responded, unfastening my belt and letting the pouch and sling fall to the ground. Joab glanced at me uncertainly, unwilling to follow suit, torn between allegiance and prudence. At this point a rock hit him on the shoulder from behind. He staggered.

The lean one grinned: "Greetings from Zerah, son of Tahath of Benjamin! You are trespassing on our mountain. Prepare to die."

More stones flew at us from behind, some scoring hits. Our opponent's rear guard had melted around the hill and taken us by surprise. We were in disarray, disadvantaged, and about to be engulfed.

"Flee!" I yelled, grabbing my fallen pouch and sling and racing away, closely followed by Joab and the rest. Jeers and taunts followed us, along with our pursuers. Abishai fell back and ran awkwardly in another direction.

"Smite the cripple!" ordered the lean captain, coming to a halt while he reloaded his sling.

Two of their number pursued the unfortunate Abishai. Their whole group came to a halt to watch the smiting.

"Keep running!" I commanded my flagging troops. I knew Abishai – he was creating a diversion to enable us to make more distance. He dodged uncomfortably from rock to rock while our adversaries howled derision. I stopped, ready to run to his assistance, Joab beside me. We both started to run back.

Assistance was not necessary, however: all of a sudden the cripple turned into a warrior, and it became clear who was going to smite, and who was going to be smitten. Abishai smote the two boys very competently, then leapt nimbly away and came cantering towards us like a war-horse with tail erect. The lean captain howled profanities and led a charge down the hill after the three of us. We led them a merry dance away from the path our comrades had taken, and as we drew closer to our own hills they fell away and were lost to our eyes.

*

"I know what I want," said Joab, later, as Asahel inspected his bruised shoulder in our valley. "I want vengeance. What was that Benjamin pig's name? Zerah. We will arrange a second meeting. I will organise it."

"You will? How will you do that?"

Joab gazed at me darkly. He felt his shoulder: "Do we not know his name? Do we not know his father's name? I will do it. Do not wonder how I will do it. It will be done."

*

So, here we were, several months later, at the end of the grape harvest. We had an appointment with destiny: an appointment that we both looked forward to and dreaded. The lean boy and his band were to meet us on the hill of Aroeah this very day – but we were a smarter outfit than at our last meeting, and we knew who we were up against. I had appointed Joab as our commander, and in the previous months we had trained: we had competed in fighting and in war games

49

– and had become a well-oiled unit. This was mostly Joab's doing, and in the process of preparation I had learned much from him. Little did I know how valuable this education was to be for me in later years, for I was to be a man of war, a man of blood, and a leader of men. But now, right now, I was young and untried and about to go into battle (thanks to Joab) – against a hardened and deceptive enemy.

So off we went, with our clubs and our slings, leaving the safety of our homes, and heading towards the inhospitable high hills that bordered Benjamin and Judah. A distant city came into view on our left, with the early morning sun glancing off its flat rooftops. A city on a hill. We arrived early at the battlefield and immediately began putting our strategy into action. There were two elevated rocky mounds at either end of a flat plain which was about two hundred paces long. One mound was to be our base, the other the enemy's. In the centre of the plain we built two cairns, fifty paces apart with stones spaced between them. This was the battleline.

There were twenty of us. Michael had been sent home by Joab shortly after we left, along with my harp.

"We are not going to sing to them," Joab had pointed out. As for Michael, he was deemed too fine and timid for this kind of adventure.

"We don't need you. You can write about our victory when we return with the spoil," Joab told him.

The timid one had not argued; if anything, he looked relieved, and this instruction of Joab's defined Michael's role for the future. He learnt to read and to write and became a man not of war, but of letters. In this respected capacity – for scribes were highly esteemed – he was to serve me faithfully for many years, in fact a lifetime. He became a recorder of the events of my youth and manhood, and a preserver of the many songs to God that I composed and sang. He studied under Ishpah, as I did, and was a gifted student. Joab too learned to read and write. He recognised the advantage it would bring him. But not everyone was literate. Farming and warfare were the staples of our lives, and you could swing a mattock or a battle-axe without learning how to read.

We gathered at our rocky camp and surveyed the terrain. It was a fine, cold autumn day, and the rocks acted as a shelter. There was no sign of the bullies – we were early, and this was part of our battle plan, since there was preparation to be done and strategy to put in place. First, a lookout was stationed at a high point to alert us to the enemy's approach. Then Abishai and six picked boys, including Amasa, were detailed to a hiding place behind the enemy's base: Joab planned to catch them out as they had done to us. Rocks were prepared, all was made ready. The lookout signalled the approach, and soon enough the cocky bullies appeared in the distance – twelve of them – and headed towards us. We watched them keenly, keeping an eye on our lookout, who would alert us if there was a second band waiting in reserve: arms spread out like an eagle meant no reserves; arms vertical meant – beware. The eagle sign was given and relayed to Abishai, who was heading our ambush. We watched as the bullies got set up. It was time to fight. Showtime.

"For David and Judah!" we cried in unison – and fired a pitiful volley of stones at the enemy, most of which fell short of the battleline. Shouts of derision greeted this feeble showing and all twelve of the bullies stepped forward, out of the cover of the rocks. "Like lambs to the slaughter," Joab muttered, through gritted teeth. We reloaded. Zerah, the lean leader, arrived unarmed at the battleline at the head of his untrained rabble, to utter a challenge. I wondered if it was to be a challenge to single combat, then I remembered how Abishai had dealt with two of their number on the last occasion; they wouldn't have forgotten that. Single combat was not on the menu for today.

Zerah preceded his comments with a few oaths. Then: "Are you ready, little boys?" he taunted: "… or do you want to run home like good little lambs, before the nasty wolf comes to tear you?" His followers sniggered.

Zerah warmed to his theme: "We are going to send you home with broken bones… all your clubs and slings will become ours. How dare you face us, the wolves of Benjamin! You are very silly boys. Quick! Run! We will count to fifty. There is still time to run away, little boys."

I was amazed at the effect Zerah's words were beginning to have on our morale. I could sense our unity and confidence being stolen away by his insidious stuff. I sensed it was time to act, but Joab pre-empted me:

"Fire!" he cried, with magnificent confidence.

Crash! Crash! Crash! Rocks fell around the bullies, and this time – it was a volley with a vengeance. Those that were hit yelped with pain. All were taken by surprise and disconcerted. We saw our advantage.

"For David and Judah, charge!"

And in we went, clubs flailing. Six bullies were on the ground in submission, the other six scampered back to their rocks for their weapons, only to be set upon by Abishai's squad, who had taken possession of their camp. It was all over. Well – nearly.

Only Zerah was unsubmitted. Truly, he did have the look of a wolf, as he snarled at us with his back to a wall of rock. He changed his club from hand to hand.

"YOU!" he burst out, glaring at Joab with unrepressed hatred. "You lied to me. You said it would be twelve against twelve, you dead dog's head!" He threw in a few foul oaths for good measure.

Our captain's eyes narrowed: "And you believed me, O Wise One? Where are your troops? Where is your victory? Where is your wisdom? Go home! Chop wood, carry water, take yourselves away. Crawl back to where you came from! Leave your clubs, and your rocks, and your slings, and be grateful for today's lesson. Next time, it will be bitter."

Zerah's expression changed as conflicting thoughts ran through his mind. His eyes dropped to the ground for a moment and he stopped changing his club from hand to hand. In that moment, Joab, son of Zeruiah, struck. He hurled his club at the lean one, and it caught him on the chest and shoulder with a sickening crack. Zerah crumpled like twigs underfoot, and his followers breathed a collective sigh of horror as they beheld the violent assault. This might soon be their lot, too.

Joab looked at me in a peculiar way. The look said without words: "I have fulfilled my duty. Now you take over." It was a look that I was destined to see many times in the years to come. I stepped forward. My mind raced; how should I finish this? With violence and intimidation, thus creating fertile ground for an ongoing feud – as if we did not have enough enemies? And in fact, these bullies of Benjamin, were they not our brothers? Would not we be fighting one day side by side against the Philistines, or against Moab, or Edom, or

Amalek? What would Ishpah do? What would Michael recommend? Our fallen foes watched me apprehensively, waiting to learn their fate.

"Listen, brothers of Benjamin," I began. "This day you have been outwitted and beaten, and you are in our power, with none to deliver."

I paused to see what effect my words might be having. There was no response; but they all sensed that I was leading up to something peaceful and magnanimous, and they began to look relieved and hopeful. My own troops had the same feeling, but not all appeared too happy about it, especially the sons of: you-know-who.

"You've been beaten," I repeated: "… and outwitted. We could do evil to you if we wished; but we do not wish." Twelve pairs of Benjamin eyes looked at me with the beginnings of hope, even affection, in their frightened gaze. Actually, eleven pairs. Zerah was not looking at me: the lean wolf had eyes for another, and there was no love lost in his gaze. But he was out of contention; hurt and alone.

"We do not wish to do you evil," I intoned. "You are our brothers. We share the same heritage, we share the same God. One day we will fight for each other, not against each other. Now gather your stuff and return home, three by three. You three first."

The first three obeyed eagerly. They showed respect, and gratitude was in their eyes as they crossed their hands on their chests and bowed, before setting off.

"Should we not at least break their arms?" demanded Abishai: "We are the victors after all. Are we really going to let them get off scot-free?" There was a murmur of assent from some of our party.

"Well – at least take their weapons!" suggested Amasa.

A rumble of agreement followed this, and the vanquished hesitated. They were quite ready to surrender their weapons if it meant a free pass to safety; but I could afford to be merciful.

"Are we not brothers?" I repeated: "Are we not of the same blood? Let it be as I have said; it is better this way. Trust me."

The vanquished scuttled eagerly away, three by three. Last to go was Zerah and his two chief henchmen. He hobbled between them in great discomfort of both body and spirit, muttering dark revenges under his breath. We watched them out of sight – it was over.

"What now, O Wise One?" Joab enquired, caustically: "Now that we have watched Benjamin escape in peace, so that he can return for war – and still armed?"

"He will not return," I assured my firebrand captain: "… and if he does it will be as friend, not foe. But for us now it is fitting to give thanks to God, for victory has been ours today, and God is gracious, as we have been. Gather around."

Obediently my troops gathered around and joined me in a song of praise and thanks, one of many that we had learned, handed down from generation to generation.

"I will sing unto the Lord, for he has triumphed gloriously, the horse and rider thrown into the sea.

The Lord, my God, my strength, my song, is now become my victory."

We sang as we had been taught, and as our spirits led us to sing, and that day on a cold hilltop in Judah, there was warmth and comradeship and closeness to God.

"Next time..." Joab commented humorously, but sincerely: "...next time we go to battle, we *will* bring the harp."

He glanced at me with a mixture of reverence and admiration that told me his allegiance was secure, even if my ways were not his.

"But..." he added: "... we will still leave Michael behind."

This unexpected droll remark somehow caused the whole party to disintegrate into laughter. It was the tension dissipating I suppose. We stayed on that hilltop until the shadows lengthened: singing, dancing, eating our simple rations, basking in the glory of our mighty deeds and in our comradeship – and in the wonder of creation on all sides.

Chapter 5
Zizi and Didi

Pomegranates…

I loved pomegranates.

All through summer they fruited, and our large family had several trees, which we guarded and tended jealously, often camping out under a rough shelter to keep an eye on them in peak periods. Woe betide any thief who pinched our pomegranates… especially while my sister Zeruiah was on guard. Coming between a mother bear and her cubs would have been preferable. Yes, Zeruiah was a spirited woman… but all Hebrew women were. Deep down, they were all spirited women… and great dancers too, I might add. Burdened by ceaseless toil, fighting for their families' survival, in subjection to their husbands, bearing up against the harshness of life – the wars, the famines, the cold, the heat – they were an obdurate lot: tenacious survivors. They had to be. It always amazed me how unlike the young girls the older women were: almost like a separate race. Often a woman just a few years married was already lined of face and sinewy of frame. When they argued or fought, usually in the market-place while bartering for goods, the women did it loudly and fiercely, with raised voices, theatrical gestures, imprecations

– the lot. I found these stand-offs fascinating, and would look on open-mouthed, along with other gawkers. No quarter was given; each woman was bent on the survival of her family – and if coming to an agreement meant having a blazing row – then a row they would have. Zeruiah did not belong to this type of woman, however. She quietly and energetically conducted her trading, with a deft and insightful touch. She was still handsome and lithe too, my sister, despite having three boys and no husband. So why no husband? What was the story, I wondered?

"Tell me, I have to know," I implored her one day.

"Do you really want to know?"

"I do, I really do! As the Lord lives!"

"Well…" she paused in her grinding and surveyed me with an amused yet fierce eye: "This is the account of my husband. You know the desert people? The traders? Think you that they are a beautiful people?"

I nodded. She flashed me an odd look, and I blushed, recalling my feelings for the little harp princess, the story of whom had become part of our family history by this time. She smiled: "Yes. And I found them beautiful too, especially one. This one came back to me, three years in succession, and then he did not come back."

"Why not?"

"It is not mine to know."

"What was his name?" I enquired softly.

She gazed at me quizzically and responded even more softly. "Warrior," she breathed.

I had to be satisfied with this brief explanation, because it was all I was going to get. Ishpah later gave me a different story. In his account her husband was from a village in the forest. He was a Hebrew like us, and dark and handsome. A fearsome soldier, he had followed King Saul and died in battle, under Abner's command. His grave was in Bethlehem. A few years went by before I dared test this story on my sister, and she looked at me, stroked my hair and said… nothing.

I continued to help with the grinding, rotating the upper mill wheel – it was easier with two. We were grinding dried red lentils for Esau bread, as Zeruiah called it. It would make a change from pottage. When the grinding was done the flour would be mixed with salt, seasoning, and goat's milk, and a little olive oil; then worked into dough and cooked on a flat, clay plate. I couldn't wait – I was starved, as usual.

Suddenly, I stopped grinding, and looked at the hand mill with interest. It was the usual circular design: a solid, lipped lower millstone with an exit channel, and a loosely fitting upper millstone, with a wooden handle. A vertical axle came up inside the central hole in the upper millstone. The grain was poured down this hole. The axle, swollen at the base, caused the grain to be drawn between the two wheels and ground. Then the flour trickled out of the channel into a clay bowl. But this isn't what was catching my attention. Zeruiah's mill was dull black in colour, whilst all the ones I had seen before were grey. It was heavier too; I could tell that by turning it. Also, it worked better.

"Where did you get this mill from?" I asked. "It's a beauty!"

My sister smiled a teasing smile. "My Warrior," she breathed: "It's made of the hard, black rock you find in the mountains of the desert. The grey rock is commoner, and easier to work. Actually, it's white when first cut, but it doesn't last long if you don't treat it with care. But this will last forever. I don't know how it was made, it's as hard as rock!" she added, flippantly.

At this point her three sons came in from foraging for fuel. They were starving too. It hadn't rained for two months so there was no problem getting the goat dung fire started. A few dry thorns, some donkey hair, and some careful blowing on the dormant coals, and pazooya! – flames appeared!

"Build that fire up well," Zeruiah instructed: "I want the plate hot when I return. Abishai, take over from me, I am going out and will be back."

Joab built up the fire in its hole in the earth floor, and smoke filled the dark stone hut. Abishai and myself, cross-legged on the earthen living platform, disappeared temporarily in smoke, and kept grinding. The clay bowl was almost full of flour. Asahel sat next to us on a sheepskin, lost in his own contented, childish world, with a reflective smile on his sweet face. He was seven. The fire settled down to its work, and the smoke became a column, which reached up to a high window slit, and streamed out into the brilliant, dazzling sky outside. Smoke does funny things. The pot was full.

"The pot's full!" Joab said.

"We know."

"Shake in the rest of the stuff. You'll have to lift off the upper millstone with the wedges. Here, I'll show you how." Joab and Abishai levered up the top millstone and brushed in the rest of the flour very carefully; none was to be wasted.

"Where's Ima?" complained Asahel. "Can we have something to eat now? What about some figs or even a pomegranate?"

Figs were out of the question. There were cakes and cakes of them in a stone storage jar, but these had been dried and pressed and saved up for hungrier days ahead. No one dared touch them; Zeruiah could smell guilt at twenty paces. There were other storage jars too, made of stone or pottery, standing in recesses in the walls, containing other, less appetising foods: dried beans, parched corn, wheat and barley. Also, there were oils: olive and flax. Flax oil was Zizi's pet health tonic for her bouncing boys – but there was nothing which appealed to us.

I made one of my decisions: "This is what we will do. We have a good harvest of pomegranates on Eliab's tree, and he's away with the army and might not be back for weeks. If we go and harvest the ones that need to be picked, we will be saving them from going too ripe. My father always says to be a good steward of what God has given us."

Joab looked at me in a peculiar way, but Abishai was already at the door: "What are we waiting for?" he demanded.

We soon returned with our booty – ten perfect pomegranates, as large as grapefruits. "Amazing, isn't it?" I meditated: "How the pomegranate tree can grow on a dry, barren, stony hill and still produce these succulent fruits. Listen! I've got an idea. Let's press them into juice – and fill the jug and hide it. Then when your mother comes, we can share the drink – a surprise! Let's break them up and squeeze them into that big pot."

Down to work we got, dismantling the fruit and squeezing the bright red seeds. "I've got a better idea," said Asahel, with his mouth full of pomegranate: "Let's use the mill!"

"Alright!" Joab agreed: "… let's take all the skins off and feed the seeds through the mill. Be quick! We need to finish before Ima returns."

"Are you sure this will work?" asked Abishai.

"Of course!"

Our hunger forgotten in the heat of the moment, we worked as one. I carried the skin and the pulp outside to the courtyard for the donkey, who had been watching us inquisitively from the door. He nosed at the pulp with an offended air and stamped his back hoof. Back inside, the boys were making a brand-new scientific experiment, pushing wet seeds down the central shaft of the hand mill, and expecting a river of pure juice to issue forth. I looked on with interest.

"It's not working! Turn the handle the other way."

"What difference will that make?"

"I can't turn it, it's jammed!"

"I told you this would happen. Wait till Ima sees this!"

"Whatever are you doing?" A fine, resonant female voice penetrated our awareness with a beautiful but dangerous timbre. Ima of the flashing eyes had returned.

"We are making you a pomegranate juice as a surprise," I explained quickly.

"And you are using my flour mill?"

Four scared pairs of eyes waited and watched as Zeruiah took stock of the situation. What would she do? Would it be dire? I watched as the three boys prepared themselves for their fate – and admired their stalwart character. Their mother investigated the large pot of juice and seeds and sifted it with a wooden spoon that I had once made her.

"Are these from Eliab's trees?" she enquired, shrewdly.

We nodded.

She smiled. "They're bound to be missed, but not to worry. So, you call this a surprise?"

We nodded.

"This is indeed a surprise, a lovely surprise, and I thank you all so much – especially you, Didi. You are such a wonderful influence on the boys! Come to me, all of you, for a lovely hug! I'm such a blessed woman, to come home for such a beautiful and delicious treat."

Any traces of sarcasm were quite lost on Asahel, who idolised his mother. He quickly came for his hug, followed by his brothers. We all returned to the fray. Joab and Abishai to clean out the mill – and me and Asahel back to the squeezing. A little later we were all sharing Esau cakes and pomegranate juice – with pips. It is the most exquisite and healthful drink in creation.

"Something you need to know, and I will tell you, is about to fall from my lips," Zeruiah announced, rather obscurely, at the end of this occasion:

"Had you tried this idea out on any normal hand mill, you would have ruined it. The juice would have stained and permeated the stone, making it soft and pasty. You are fortunate that my hand mill is made from the black rock of the mountains. You have my warrior to thank for this," she breathed.

*

Zizi (that was my pet name for Zeruiah) lived outside the little town of Bethlehem, as did many others. Her one room home was simple: thick stone walls plastered with mud and lime, a roof of earth and wood and a small, walled courtyard.

The living and the sleeping were done on the raised earth platform farthest from the door. The door itself was made of sticks, hanging vertically, which could be tied back to keep open, or untied to close. A heavy goat-hair blanket helped to keep the cold out when necessary, which it often was. Bethlehem was perched high in the Judean hills. We got snow and rain in winter and wind all year round. Mind you – it could get hot in the middle of the day, even in spring and autumn, especially when the hot desert wind – the sirocco – blew in from the southeast. We thought it was hot, but it was nothing like Jericho, apparently. Down there, in the Jordan valley, a mere day's journey away, it was steaming hot all summer – or so I was told.

I liked the hills.

Zizi was my confidante. From her I learnt much of our history, and it was of great interest to me. Ten generations previously, our nation had spent forty years wandering in the desert. We had arrived in this land of milk and honey only ten generations ago. It was our Promised Land: promised by God to our ancestor Abraham, many, many generations ago. How many, I wanted to know? Well, around thirty generations, Zeruiah reckoned. And how many years would that have been, I wondered? Hmmm… maybe seven or eight hundred. So, a lot of history to uncover. Who built Bethlehem? I wanted to know – and why was it so small and so crowded?

"How would *you* like to build a wall around a town?" was the cryptic answer. Bethlehem was a walled town, with a single gate. It was built by the previous inhabitants – the Canaanites.

"So – what happened to them? Where did they go?" I enquired.

Zeruiah shook her head at me kindly: "Didi, you are such an innocent…"

Building a wall was a massive task for anyone, she explained, even when rocks were readily available, so people always built a wall that was as short in length as possible. This resulted in small towns, sometimes less than a bow-shot across, as in our case. As time went on more and more people built within the town, until it became a maze of narrow passages, with houses on houses, houses in the walls, houses everywhere. This was great for hide and seek but… the smells were unpleasant… and it could get really muddy! But it was not as bad as other nations, since we had our own strict rules for hygiene and for washing. Each family had a special spade, for example. But still – there were no bathrooms or running water. So – what with donkeys, camels, lambs and goats nosing around – not to mention people – and dogs – I'll leave it to your imagination. The worst times would have been when under siege from enemies. That hadn't happened to me yet, and it didn't bear thinking of. Then, everyone from the nearby countryside would flee to the town – doubling its population – with no opportunity to go out. This is why we needed an army, Zeruiah pointed out: to keep this from happening – and let us thank God for Saul, our king, whose whole life seemed to be engaged in fighting our enemies; and thanks for Eliab, my brother, and those like him, who protected our people.

"Why is the well outside the town?" I wanted to know.

"What do you mean? Where else would the well be?"

"Inside the town. Then, if we are under siege we will have water. Otherwise, we all die of thirst while our enemy watches and drinks our water."

Zizi nodded reflectively: "You have a good point. However, if the well was within the walls our lives would become impossible with all the herds to water and only one gate. It would be a nightmare! But then again – if we were locked inside the walls with no water, then yes, we would all die of thirst, eventually. That's not so clever, is it? What we need is a tunnel from within to give us access to the water. I will talk to father about this."

Our father – Jesse – son of Obed, son of Boaz (who married Ruth the Moabitess) – was one of the village elders. He was already old when I, the last of his children, was born. The home I grew up in within the walls of Bethlehem was one of the originals from the previous owners. It was much better built than the basic sort of homes our tribe was able to build. After all, we had been slaves and desert dwellers and nomads in our previous history – and had therefore brought few building skills with us. True, our forefathers had had plenty of experience when it came to making mud bricks for Pharaoh – as well as shaping stones and hauling blocks and making rope out of flax and papyrus: but this was as slaves under whips. Little of this know-how was handed down.

My father's home was close to the gate and backed onto the wall of the town. It was three storeys high, with two rooms on each floor. Beneath the ground level, a cistern had been hollowed out of the soft rock and lined with mortar. It had a narrow top and was shaped like a fat bottle. The rainwater from our roof ran into this cistern, and the water was valuable for washing, and for the animals – but not for drinking, except in extreme situations. If I went onto the roof, away from the noise and smells of the streets below, I could walk along the town wall and look out over the hills and forests. I was often on the flat roof, but not just for looking. It was a good place to sleep in summer. It was also where figs, flax and grapes were dried, and where family gatherings took place with stories and songs, and sometimes the women took their spinning and weaving up there.

A low wall ran around the edge of the roof for safety, as God's law required. A favourite game for children was to run around this wall as fast as possible without falling off the building. In this way we overturned God's safety measures, without realising we were doing so. Also, we played catch from one wall to the other, with a dried pomegranate. When we played teams at this game, the action was fast and furious. Three jump-downs and you were out. Such activities usually took place before the evening meal, since the rest of the day we were busy. My mother was not keen on this game. She said it was bad for the wall – which it was – but my father enjoyed it and came up especially to watch – also to stop it when things started to get out of hand.

One of my jobs, in fact one of every boy's job when growing up, was to look after the roof and keep it from leaking. Roofs were made by placing beams from wall to wall, then cross-hatching them with branches and brushwood, and adding clay and mud and cut grass and straw. Essentially, a roof was one great, reinforced, clay tile… not exactly flat, but rising towards the centre so the water would run to the edges and follow a channel to the exit point, which in our case could also be diverted to the underground cistern. Maintaining this kind of a roof was an art. Since the rain constantly eroded and took the mud away, the roof had to be replenished with new mortar; soft spots had to be found and fixed, and any leaks repaired as well. Without attention, a roof could suffer extreme damage in just one winter, so, along with every other boy in our world, I had to fill my leather bucket with dirt, climb up the outer stone stairway to the roof and upkeep it. Joab, three years my junior, was expert at this task by the time he was ten. He had a natural aptitude for all the tasks and challenges our culture presented, plus he knew how to instruct and delegate. Well, that's enough about him… for now.

Each roof had its own stone roller which resided permanently on the roof. The roller was an arm-length in width and a handspan in height. To keep the roof smooth, suitable mortar of a certain dampness (not too sticky, not too dry) had to be broadcasted and screeded, then rolled. This form of maintenance had to be kept up whenever necessary, otherwise the roof would leak and a drip could quickly become a torrent. "Living with a nagging wife," my father occasionally intoned: "… is like sitting under a constant dripping on a very rainy day."

Why he said this I have no idea, since my mother was the quietest and most industrious wife in Bethlehem, and she and my father were deeply in love all of their days. It was a proverb, this saying, and my father had a large store of proverbs, handed down from posterity, which he used when he saw fit. Perhaps he was just reminding me to check the roof. I sometimes used to think about some of our proverbs: "Many a man proclaims his steadfast love, but a faithful man who can find?" Now what did that mean, I wondered? And: "A gentle answer turns away wrath." That was easier to understand, but not often practiced. I planned to do it, however: any way I could find, to become wiser and more Godly – and more like Joseph my hero – I would do it.

Chapter 6
The Day of the Shepherd

Seasons rolled by – and childhood – with all its excitement and wonders, and fun and adventures, and fears – rolled by with it. Now other children played hide and seek… and ran and wrestled and play-acted, and skipped, and did chores and listened to stories at night, and hid behind their mother's skirts. For me, childhood was fleeting away, and I entered my teenage years. The years of longing, the years of apartness, of yearning and of new-found sensuality… these years arrived. It was a sensuality keenly felt and unfulfilled. Sweet and summoning, insatiable and unattainable. Powerful and undeniable.

I was glad to be a shepherd in the hills, and no longer a Bethlehem boy. My role of leader had been taken over by, well, who else? Joab, of course. But for me, seasons of solitude and soul-searching had come. A shepherd's life suited me very well. It was hard but not burdensome, except at shearing time, or so I had heard, and life beneath the sun and the stars had an eternal, ageless, timeless feeling that my spirit loved. I felt like a star thrown through the ages in a fiery trail. I could sense the presence of our ancestors in these very hills; Joseph, Judah, Jacob, Samson… I dreamt of them and my dreams were powerful and sustaining, and I sensed God's presence with me; His wings overshadowing me.

A shepherd's job was to look after his sheep: to feed and water them, to lead them, to call them each by name, and to talk to them. At night the various flocks on the mountains mingled together in the rough stone sheepfolds that had been maintained for generations. These were simply walls, and sheep went in with sheep, and goats with goats. On cold nights, we slept alongside the sheep for warmth. This was why the Egyptians hated the Israelites in the days of Jacob: because we were shepherds and we stunk. And yet – one of Jacob's sons became the governor of all Egypt. As for me, I'd sooner be warm – and the smell isn't that bad – you can always wash.

In the early morning the shepherds would tap their sticks and utter their own peculiar calls, and the sheep and goats would go to their own shepherd and follow him. In this way, purely by calling and tapping, a mass of sheep would divide neatly into their separate flocks and set off for the day's grazing. At night, we regathered. We had fires for cooking. Bread and mountain goat stew with herbs and goat's milk cheese was our favourite fare – but more often than not we had to be content with less. Meat was in short supply, since our herd animals were not for food and had to be strictly accounted for to the families who owned them. So meat, when we got it, was either mountain goat, or gazelle, or birds such as partridge or quail. Some shepherds carried bows and snares, but slings were the most convenient weapon.

Slings were easy to carry and ammunition was readily available. They were also a handy shepherding tool: a well-placed rock could head off and redirect an errant sheep or two. My leather sling had worn out by now and Zeruiah had plaited me a new one out of flax. She loved the flax plant, did Zizi – for cloth, for rope, and for oil – and she traded vigorously in the marketplace for supplies. Most of our flax came from Jericho. My new sling was infinitely superior to my old one, and I practiced diligently, as did the other shepherds. Bringing down a mountain goat was a rare feat, requiring great accuracy and power. I must admit, I achieved this feat on several occasions, much to the amazement of other shepherds, who were a rough bunch, and not easily impressed. The tools of a shepherd's trade were few: a club, a knife, a sling, a pouch for tinder, a bag for flour, a staff, sandals, a hooded cloak, and in my case, a harp. Also – a reed pipe provided a convenient musical diversion for many. Oh yes, and of course – a goat-hide wineskin.

Goats – they were such vital creatures to our survival. The surrounding nations even had goat idols. The skin of a goat made an excellent bottle – for water or wine. The hide was stripped off whole, scraped, salted, re-inverted and tied off with strong flaxen thread or goat-hide thonging. The sealed-off bag was a durable container which made a good pillow at night (and this also helped to prevent theft and pilfering from other shepherds). The neck was carefully fashioned for pouring and could be opened and closed with a drawstring. After a couple of harvests, wineskins would become stretched and brittle and no longer suitable for precious wine. At this time, they would become water containers or seed containers, or even throw cushions stuffed with chaff or wool. The goat hair was often shaved off and the skins rubbed with olive oil or linseed oil (from the flax plant), or with fat; this increased their lifespan by protecting them from the elements and nourishing the thin leather. A water-skin was a vital and valuable possession, without which a shepherd's life in the harsh Judean hills would have been impossible.

During the early days of my shepherding apprenticeship, I made friends with one of the dogs that lived on the edge of town. Nimrod, I called him: Mighty Hunter. He wasn't a typical outskirts dog – mangy and quarrelsome – but a handsome, well-made dog with a sense of self-respect. He kept apart from the endless bickering of his kind – and kept a watchful eye out for me. Often, shepherds were accompanied by dogs: they make useful sentries. Some of them are natural sheep-dogs and keep the flock in good formation as they graze on the mountainsides. When Nimrod was in charge, all I had to do was find an elevated place to watch from. He was well worth the occasional treat and titbit.

One sunny day I was watching over my flock – all ten of them – with Nimrod, my trusty helper, when in the distance I saw a runner heading in our direction. He ran in a way that I recognised. It was Ethan, my old follower, who was now a servant of my father, and very grateful to be in service to such a kind master. Camouflaged on the mountainside, I was difficult to spot, so I flashed my copper knife in the sun until he noticed. Then he headed directly for us and ran even harder. What was going on, I wondered? I was expecting more provisions, but not for another day or two, and anyway, Ethan was empty-handed. A wild assortment of thoughts and images filled my mind: a raid, a siege, Philistines, Amalekites, Edomites? Should I run to meet him? Better not – that would disturb the sheep. I gathered my things and walked down to where the flock was grazing – and waited.

"What news?" I demanded.

Ethan halted, and leant with his hands on his knees, gasping. "Good news," he gasped. He gazed at me with that peculiar shy smile that I remembered well from boyhood: "Your father wishes you to return home now, this minute, to Bethlehem, without delay and immediately."

"For what reason?"

"I know not."

"Then why is it good news?"

"I know not."

"Then will I bring the sheep?"

"Absolutely not! I will attend to them until your return. But you must hasten. Run! Now!"

Questions flooded my mind, but there was no time for them. My course of action was clear. I ran. Nimrod watched me go with an alert and understanding air, as if he knew better than me what this was all about. The sheep looked alarmed and flighty, but a quick 'keep grazing' growl from Nimrod, and their calm was restored. I ran.

As I leapt down the mountainsides and along the valleys, my spirit leapt within me. I felt free, like a bird in flight. I carried my sandals; they were precious to me and I didn't want to damage them in my headlong flight, and as long as I didn't dash my foot against a stone, or discover a thorny branch, then I could run like the wind. It was a hazardous mission, since rocks and thorns abound in the Promised Land. I still hadn't come across those rivers of milk, or of honey, but I was guided by angels and keen eyes, and reached the outskirts of Bethlehem just before midday.

Strangely for that hour of the day – there were people standing around. As I arrived, Zeruiah, my father's strong right hand, stepped forward and beckoned me.

"Come! Follow me," she instructed. She led me inside her home, where she exchanged my rough, shepherd's robe for a linen tunic, and washed my hands and face, having first given me some food and drink, for I was faint.

"Come," she repeated, ignoring my questions, and led me through the town to the altar of sacrifice, where a group of elders stood. A thought flashed through my mind. Isaac! Was I to be offered as a sacrifice? Me? Sacrificed?

Ridiculous, unworthy thought, begone! Other nations did such things, but not our nation. Zizi stopped at a respectful distance from the elders, along with some other villagers, and looked on. I was dimly aware of my brothers in the throng, and the looks on their faces of puzzlement, resentment, curiosity, scorn – the usual looks. I was also aware of the eyes of the elders upon me, and of my father, as I went forward; but most of all, far and away, I was aware of the eyes of another man, one whom I had never seen before, but whom I knew immediately. He was older than my father, dressed in an ancient silvery-grey hooded robe. He leant on a staff. He had silver eyebrows and a compelling visage – deep brown eyes and a steady gaze – and he emanated meekness and power, and the Spirit of God. He had eyes for no one but me.

"Is this the one? Let him come before me."

I knelt before him, my father's hand upon my shoulder.

"Look at me," the old man intoned, removing his hood.

I gazed obediently into the eyes of Samuel, who had been the judge and prophet of Israel since my father's youth, and as I did so I felt lifted up in my heart and in my spirit… lifted up into heavenly places… lifted up into new and unimaginable realms. Am I floating? I asked myself. Are my feet still on the ground? I'm sure they weren't, but the deep, compelling, yet restful eyes of the prophet held me still. Whole seconds passed. Eternities.

"This is the one," Samuel stated quietly, and in the hush that had fallen on the assembly, every word was clear. "He is not great of stature, though one day he may be so. He is not a proven warrior, nor of any great account in Israel. He is not yet a full-grown man, but God does not look upon the outward appearances of a man. Strength and power to God are but weakness and frailty. God looks on the heart. Our god, Yahweh, looks on the heart, and you – young man – have a heart after God – a heart of integrity and worship. Never lose it… Hold that heart close and dear, it is your most precious possession, for out if it flow the wellsprings of life. God has chosen you, David, son of Jesse of Bethlehem, to be the king of his people, Israel, in a time that he will choose. Kneel before the presence of our God," he murmured to the onlookers.

The circle of elders knelt as one man. The outer circle of watchers too.

"I now anoint you David, son of Jesse, in the name of the Name… of Yahweh, our Lord and our Deliverer… in accordance with his will – to be king, in his sight, over his people, Israel. Selah. Amen and Amen. Be it done according to your will, O Lord our God."

The horn of oil was poured liberally over my youthful head, my hair glistening redly in the sun (as Zeruiah later told me) and the warm flow trickled down my forehead and my neck, down my nose and chin, and onto my garments, like the dew of Mount Hermon. I raised my eyes once more to the Prophet Samuel, and there I read untold tales of struggle, and of overcoming, and of loss, and of attainment, and of faithful loyalty to the One. But most of all I discerned strength and belief in his eyes: strength in the Lord, and belief in His ways.

"What shall I do?" I whispered.

Samuel looked at me in a way I still remember – and gave me an answer I thought I would never forget: "Guard your heart," he said.

*

Later that afternoon I made my way back into the mountains. After the ceremony a white heifer had been sacrificed, incense burnt, and prayers and songs lifted up to heaven. In all of this I had felt separate – as if in another world. When the time came for the prophet to go, he blessed me – then the people gathered outside the gate to honour his departure.

All of a sudden, I knew that this was a time in my life when I wanted to be alone with God. I was conscious of a stirring in my heart; I felt lifted up by the Spirit. I glanced at Ishpah, my teacher, whose burning eyes glowed with wonder and amazement and understanding, then took my leave of my father and returned to the hills. My heart was full that day.

My way led me past the ancient, hollow, olive trees that still yielded fruit each season, and there were birds flashing about the red flowers of the sage plants underneath. As they came to each flower they hovered in mid-air, with wings a blur. I marvelled at the beauty of God's creation all around me and fell to my knees and raised my hands and my face to Heaven. Joy flooded through me; the boundless joy of being in the hands and purposes of the One who had called me. "The Lord has called you to shepherd his people, Israel. To be his leader in a time of his choosing," the prophet had said, loudly and clearly, in the hearing of all. Everybody knew. At the same time, everybody knew to keep quiet about it, lest word should reach King Saul. He would not relish such news.

I left the path and lay down among the sage plants, in the shadow of the olives. The birds darting and hovering were long beaked and smartly attired in buff and black and white plumage. As I lay there, hidden among the foliage, sleep came over me, and when I woke up, the sun was low on one side of the sky, and a full moon was rising on the other. In my dream I had been sitting at the feet of Samuel, (or was it Ishpah?) and over and over the soft words were repeated, like a song, like water running in a brook: "Guard your heart, walk in integrity. Guard your heart, walk in integrity…" Visions of the two faces stayed with me as I wended my long and silent way back to the sheepfolds. When I got there the moon was high and the mountains and rocks were bathed with moonlight.

"It is I, David, son of Jesse," I called out to the sentries as I approached, and Nimrod came bounding down the track and frisked about me. I joined the company beside the fire and was given some lentil stew that had a faint taste of meat about it, together with some ancient, rock-hard bread, and a piece of old cheese. "A meal fit for a king!" one of the shepherds commented. This comment, so innocently and opportunely made, somehow tickled my sense of humour, and once I started laughing, I found it hard to stop.

"What happened to you today?" Ethan enquired, curiously. "You look different."

"Everything is fine," I assured him, and placed my fingers to my lips. The next morning, before he left, I told Ethan what had happened to me. I knew that he would not rest until he had found out – and I was confident of his discretion.

One person I would dearly love to have had with me right now, was Michael. Little Michael, my confidant. But alas, he was no longer in my sphere of company. Only a few weeks previously he had been conscripted. King Saul's minions had scoured the countryside looking for new recruits for the King's army and for his entourage: bakers, cooks, dressmakers and perfumers from among the daughters of Israel, and men of war, slaves, farmers and ministers from among the sons. Poor Michael; not to be imagined as a soldier or a minister, and so unsuited to slavery! I wondered if I would see him again.

In the early morning of that day, my first day of being the king in waiting, I found myself overlooking the sheep next to my favourite spring. Water bubbled out of the mountainside and fanned out into a shallow pool, then disappeared back into the ground. I was lucky to have this oasis to myself this day since waterholes were few and far between in the high country. The grass was well cropped and springy. It was a joy to walk on. Birds flitted discreetly among the rocks and plants, lizards darted among the caves, bees droned, butterflies dipped and soared. High above, eagles hung in the clear, blue sky. Lions and bears, wolves and leopards prowled unseen among the tongues of forest that reached up the ravines. Brigands and bandits roamed these hills. Being a shepherd wasn't just about following sheep. As I meditated on my new responsibilities in life, my spirit became weighed down. Was I equal to all this? At this point in my life my job was to shepherd my earthly father's sheep and to protect them from harm – and soon I would have to shepherd my Heavenly

Father's sheep; the human sheep of the tribe of Israel. Who is going to look after *me*? Who is going to be *my* shepherd? Who will take over from Zizi my sister and Jesse my father?

As I wondered, my senses, attuned to danger, and ever alert, suddenly woke me from my meditations and catapulted me into the present. One of the lambs was nosing curiously at the mouth of a cave. The mother snickered plaintively, but the senseless little creature paid no attention. Why are sheep so stupid? The lamb ventured into the cave a little further. The next instant there was a noise… WOOOMPH… and the little back legs disappeared into the cave, like a shot from a sling, into the embrace of who knows what horror.

A wolf? A bear? A bandit?

Several things happened all at the same time in the next few seconds. Firstly, I wished I hadn't sent Nimrod off with Ethan: his nose would have forewarned me. Secondly, I was seized by a massive wave of anger and outrage. And thirdly, I put down my harp and grabbed my club. In the same instant I bounded down the hillside and arrived at the entrance to the cave and glared into it. At first there was nothing to be seen. Then my eyes adjusted – and I saw it: a bear.

A bear!

In a flash I was upon it and clubbed it soundly on the head. The lamb dropped from its mouth, and I caught a leg and threw the little creature out of the cave in one smooth motion. The startled bear, dispossessed of its prey and stunned from the blow, roared, reared up on its hind legs and lashed out at me, its claws grazing my shoulder. Such was the force of the strike that I found myself thrown to the side of the cave and half-stunned. I twisted and spun, found my balance again, grasped the club in both hands and swung it with deadly intent. The blow, thank God, caught my attacker on the side of the head, and it must have hit him in a sensitive spot, for he crumpled to the ground in a furry heap. I added some more blows until I was sure he was dead, then staggered out in shock, into the serene sunshine, shaking like a leaf, to collapse on the soft, green turf. The sheep looked on without interest, as if there was nothing much going on in their lives, and I noted to my relief that the young one was back with its mother and suckling, despite its ordeal. Exhaustion and relief overcame me. When I woke up again, imagine my surprise to find myself in the midst of a sea of sheep – and a large group of my fellow shepherds.

"Is that your bear?" one of them demanded, with a grin. It was Ishi, the same one who had made the 'meal fit for a king' comment the previous night. "He'll make a good meal!" he observed. "Do you want to keep the skin?"

"I do," I acknowledged.

That night, and for several nights to come, bear stew was on the menu for my fellow shepherds – but for me it was not, even if it did smell good. Our law was clear about what we could and could not eat, and if an animal had cloven hooves and chewed its cud, then you could eat it. If not, you couldn't. I had a strong desire to get things right. To guard my heart. To walk in integrity. I had Joseph to model myself on, Samuel and Ishpah to live up to, Michael to impress, and our Sovereign God to serve and honour and obey. So – it was lentils and hard cheese for me.

The next day, the day after my encounter with the bear, I returned to my mountain oasis, and after having first checked the caves for unwanted occupants, spent a few precious hours in the company of my Lord. "Who will be my shepherd?" I asked again. "Who will look after me?"

I must admit, I thought I knew the answers – but the Lord revealed more to me on that day, more than I would have dreamed of by myself, and he gave me a glimpse of Heaven – a shaft of light, like Jacob's ladder of angels – and his spirit gave me his assurance in words… words that I could speak and commit to memory… revelation words that would sustain and guide and strengthen me. And not me alone would they strengthen – but many of God's servants, down through the ages. Words like towering mountains, like sure foundations, like sheltering wings. You remember that wonderful statue of me that I mentioned earlier? Carved by a master sculptor? As wonderful as that statue is, so much more wonderful by ten times ten are those words that God composed for me that day, and which his spirit planted in my spirit: and here they are…

Don't rush through them. Come with me to that hidden oasis, and let His words wash over you slowly, like the water that bubbles out of the mountain. There is no rush. There is every reason to relax and take it easy. Trust me, this is the best part of my book. There is nothing better up ahead; how could there be? Here it is: from beside the oasis.

"The Lord is my shepherd, I shall not be in want.

He makes me lie down in green pastures.

He leads me beside still waters.

He restores my soul.

He guides me in paths of righteousness, for his name's sake.

Even though I walk through the valley of the shadow of death,

I shall fear no evil, for you are with me;
Your rod and your staff, they comfort me.
You prepare a table before me in the presence of my enemies,
You anoint my head with oil.
My cup… is overflowing.
Surely goodness and mercy
Will follow me – all the days of my life –
And I will dwell in the house of the Lord forever."

Next time I went home, I shared these words with Zizi.

"This is beautiful!" she said: "It's a song of the Lord! A psalm of strength and comfort. I will write it down."

And she did. First, she cut up an old, cracked wineskin. Then she wet it, rolled it out flat and let it dry – slowly. Then she copied the words out using lamp soot and oil as ink – and rubbed the skin with fat to seal and preserve it, before rolling it up and storing it in her treasure chest for safety.

That was the first psalm I ever wrote, and the beginning of my collection. I looked at old wineskins in a new way after that. They could be used as scrolls and were so much more available and less expensive than fresh, new hides. Of course, in time, I was able not only to afford new hides, but also to employ skilled scribes and secretaries to copy down my words, and to do so with fine Egyptian ink, with flourishes and colours and squiggles, and vine branches. But my favourite and dearest transcription was the one that Zeruiah transcribed that day – with lamp-black and oil, on an old, cracked-up wineskin.

AN OLIVE GROVE

Chapter 7
A Time to Learn

I settled down to my life as a shepherd and wanted nothing more. Well… one moment… I was a boy, and becoming a man, and, although the wild freedom of those days went to my head like new wine… yes, there were things I wanted, and wanted keenly. A wife, for example. Well, mainly. I was youthful and passionate; and male; and had a history of romantic and ecstatic dreams. I still carried with me the treasured memory of the nomad princess – of that one glance that stole my heart and of her breath-taking beauty – God's handiwork. And girls loved me. I could tell… It was well for me that my father was an honourable and loving patriarch, and that our family abided by the God-given laws of our nation, handed down by our forefathers. These laws were designed for our own protection. One day I knew my father would find me a wife, and that day was only a year or two, or three, away. In the meantime, I must wait.

So, my life as a shepherd became my life. For months at a time I was away, with the occasional visit from Ethan keeping me in touch with home. He brought supplies; flour, honey, wine. Honey was always abundant in those days. Our land was a paradise for bees, and if you knew where to look in the forest and among the low-lying crags, honey wasn't hard to find. Because bees were in such profusion, and because they worked so hard, their honeycombs eventually grew so big they would split, and fall apart, and spill honey and wax on the ground. As children we kept an eager eye out for this delectable treat, since our appetites were always keen, and the forest honey was amazing stuff. It made you feel invincible! Well, at least until you had too much of it; then it made you feel sick. We loved the wax as well, for making little animals and decorations and for waxing bowstrings and shields, and wooden handles on spades and axes. Also, we made candles with linen wicks. Candles were a rarity, however, and our main source of light was oil. Every home had at least one oil lamp to cast a feeble light on the dim interior. These lamps were little pottery bowls filled with flax oil or olive oil, or tallow, with a wick lying across the edge, flickering. Olive oil was a precious commodity: it was used for light, for cooking, for healing, and, of course, for anointing future kings of Israel. The olives were always the last harvest of the year, in autumn. As long as there were no raiders, or war, the olive harvest was an exciting time, especially if the harvest was big. In the Bethlehem area we had many olive trees, old and young – the old ones often hollow and twisted, but still productive – and we had a system for sharing the work and the oil so that everyone – even the poorest – would benefit from the harvest. Everyone could help and just about everyone did – including the children. That was one of their purposes in life: to help. So: beating, shaking, climbing, carting, pressing – it was continually done for several weeks, and at the end, everything was preserved and set aside for the oncoming winter. At this point we celebrated the third of our three big annual feasts: The Feast of Tabernacles.

There were a few groups of people who did not share in the olive harvest, or in the other harvests that took place during the year. Shepherds were among these groups. So, in my first year as a serious, full time shepherd, I missed out on the feasting and the dancing and the singing… and the company that went along with the yearly round. But I did not mind missing out on the digging and the tilling and the weeding and the watering. We shepherds had our own time of harvest – when the wool was collected. This was in the spring. Wine flowed, wool flew, knives flashed. It was a time of feasting and companionship. Travelling shearers came to assist with the work and for two or three weeks all was action; then the last of the donkeys, laden with wool, would disappear down the mountain track like a large, dark cloud, and it would be just us again: the shepherds, with their newly shorn sheep – and another year would begin.

I sound like I was in the mountains for years, don't I? Well – it felt like it – but in actual fact the day Samuel appeared and anointed me as the future king I had only been in the mountains for six months. I had not even participated in my first sheep shearing, except as a helper and a carrier. How I looked forward to being entrusted with a shearing knife of my own. Maybe next year.

The time I spent in the hills was a fine learning time for me. It was strange to think that there were still things to learn after having already lived fourteen action-packed years. I had been the leader of the up-and-coming new generation of Bethlehem warriors. But apparently, learning never stops. At this time, I learnt to listen to my intuition… no more camping next to bear caves… I also learnt to sleep rough and cold, to live on little, to care for my father's sheep and to judge character. This last was of great value. There was a wide range of characters out in the hills. There were shepherds who were a mixed lot, bandits and brigands, travellers, lepers, raiders… Every encounter one made could be one's last. Therefore, I learnt to pray. And – comfortingly – there was the presence of God: the God of Israel, radiant and uplifting… in the breath of the wind, in the cool light of the stars, in the rustle of the grass, in the fiery colours of the sunset – and in the distant shimmer of the Great Sea beyond.

There was a lot of space in the hill country of Judea, if you wanted it. There were a lot of wild men too. Over a period of months, I met them all in passing – and I watched them keenly. There was Cush, son of Tahath from the tribe of Benjamin, Zerah's older brother. Cush was one of King Saul's shepherds. He was a fierce and terrifying man. He made my blood run cold. What was he doing in our hills? To pass through was acceptable, provided you kept moving along, but he had planted himself here. I kept my distance. There was Sol, from Bethlehem; more than twice my age and married – a soldier and a shepherd. He was a lovely man. God appointed him to be my protector and confidant. I didn't think I needed a protector, but God thought differently. There was Ishi, of course – the joker – whose rough friendship and generosity made our occasional evening gatherings feel warm and enjoyable. There were other shepherds too. Belah, Shem, Gilead, Dan, and the list goes on. Some were independent, most were bonded slaves. Some, like me, were working for their family.

Our lives as shepherds revolved around two main concerns: water and grass. Not long after my return from my unexpected encounter with the prophet Samuel, Sol suggested we combine our flocks. He had a flock of fifty sheep and goats, I had ten. I accepted and our flocks travelled together. I still had my faithful dog Nimrod tagging along. Instinctively he included Sol's flock with mine and kept a watchful eye on all of them. Sol had been shepherding on and off for twenty years and he had an extensive knowledge of the land. Also, he was an adventurous spirit and a keen hunter, so he led me into some interesting places. One day we were beside the Oasis of En Gedi, next to the Salt Sea, and we had the place to ourselves. I had just returned from floating in the thick brine of the Sea and was washing off in the springs, when Sol hissed and pointed at something on the hillside behind me: a mountain goat. It would provide us with food for several days if only we could get it.

I stepped delicately out of the water and slipped into my rough, hooded cloak. "Keep still," he whispered. "I will go above it, behind that rock. When I call like a raven, step out and sling a rock, then be ready for whatever happens next."

"I will do so."

Sol crept up the rocky hillside, keeping out of view of our prey. The mountain goat remained stationary on its narrow ledge, scanning below. At any moment it could be gone. I took a rock from my pouch and fitted it into my sling. This was a special rock of the optimum weight: smooth and rounded, chosen with care and put aside for such a time as this. They were hard to find, such rocks. I had five of them, picked out from the dry gorge that splits the Valley of Elah. Some of the rocks in that gorge are jagged and irregular, but if you dig into the sandy deposits that occur there, you can unearth smooth, rounded stones, which fly true and hard. I fitted one into my sling and waited for the raven's call.

"How am I going to do this?" I asked myself: "If I step out into full view and start swinging this sling around my head, is the goat going to stay there? I doubt it. I shall have to swing, then step out, then release." I slipped the retaining loop over my thumb, and began circling the sling around my head, first with my right hand only, then grasped my right wrist with my left hand for power and direction and continued circling with two hands. I wanted to hit the goat right in the head – and knock it off into the springs. But this wasn't likely to happen, even though I'd been practicing, but – at least my rock would crash into the cliff face pretty close to the target – and startle our prey into action. When a mountain goat is startled it instinctively goes higher, and it is marvellous to watch them springing upward from ledge to invisible ledge, as if borne on wings. In this case, the upward path went past the rock where Sol would be hiding, intent on disabling our prospective food supply, by first breaking its legs with his club and then dispatching it with his knife. I waited, circling the loaded sling rhythmically around my head. The raven called. Two more swings to build up speed, and then I stepped sweetly into view – sighted, aimed and fired – all in one motion. The stone flew true. The goat toppled off the cliff into the springs. I leapt in and dragged it out by the horns to the rocks and drew my blade across its throat. The lifeblood drained out of it, and its struggles ceased.

I looked up just as Sol peeped around the rock to see what was happening. His face was a study when he saw. I grinned. He shook his head and laughed. "Well done young one! That was a royal shot indeed! Maybe it's you that should be looking after me!" He shook his head in disbelief and joined me down on the rocks, collecting my sling-stone on the way. Our flocks in the meantime paid no attention. They just continued chewing and grazing in sheepish indifference. Not so Nimrod: he sat at a respectful distance wagging his tail with his tongue hanging out. Our good fortune was his good fortune too.

Sol, my heaven-sent companion, opened up a new world of adventure and exploration to me. He was a brave and resourceful character: a naturalist, a soldier, a shepherd, and most of all, a survivor. He visited his home in Bethlehem only occasionally, apart from the winter months. He had two wives there, and several young children. They loved him and accepted their situation without question. Sol taught me how to make nets. I taught him how to play the harp. He played simply and boldly with a pronounced rhythm. His wives and children gathered around and danced and swayed in the sultry summer nights when we were there. They wanted to listen to me sing and would sit spellbound as the sweet notes of my nomad's harp mingled with the evening breezes. Tola was his eldest son; aged seven. He and I were good friends. It was an eternity since the day of my anointing – two months, at least. And in that time, song after song, psalm after psalm, had come to me. These were the songs Sol's family loved, and other families too.

How did I make these songs? How did I remember them? It was just like breathing. I would sit on a rock or lean on a tree and start singing to God, and the words would come. They would come like sheep appearing over a hill, like eagles descending from the sky, like lions strolling through the forest. And what were the words about? They were about God, and me, and my life, and Israel. If I felt alone, or afraid, or confused, or sick, or tired, or rejected, or full of joy and confidence and faith (which more often than not was the case) the words would come and capture my heartfelt thoughts. The wonderful thing was, that while some of these words (most of them, in fact) were my words from my own heart, some were direct from God himself – from His heart – and I didn't understand how they got into my psalms and what they meant, but they blazed like a golden sunset. Sometimes these words of God filled an entire psalm, as rain pours off a roof and fills a cistern. I was the roof, I was the cistern… and the rain was the words of God… cascading down. It was not hard for me to remember these words – they were like intimate friends – but I wrote them down nonetheless, with oil and charcoal on broken wineskins, and on stray pieces of goat hide, and hid them in the dry caves of the Judean hills in which we travelled. Most of my psalms eventually found their way to Zeruiah's treasure chest. Some may still be hidden in the caves to this day.

"Why do you do this, David my son?" Sol enquired one day.

"Do what?" I responded.

"Sit there and sing to God? Do you think He hears?"

"Of course He hears!" I laughed. "He is – 'The Great I Am, the Lord of Glory, the Father of Lights, the Creator and Sustainer of All'!"

"That is more than I expected," Sol observed, open-mouthed. "Now where did you get all those titles from?"

"Well," I said, reflecting… "I suppose it was from Ishpah. He was my teacher all those years. He taught me about the God of Israel, and he taught me how to write."

"Did he teach you how to play the harp and sing songs to God?"

"No. Not really. That just came naturally."

"And is it a good thing to do?"

"Well of course! It brings me close to God and it strengthens me. You know how in the beginning God used his voice to speak everything into being with the power of his word?"

"Yes."

"Well, when I raise my voice to God and I sing of his faithfulness and his power and praise him for his wonders and petition him for my needs… and declare my trust and hope in him… he hears my words – and he draws me close to Him and shelters me beneath his wings, and directs me, and protects me, and covers me."

Sol continued weaving linen strands into his hunting net and looking down without meeting my eyes. Eventually he looked at me thoughtfully: "You didn't eat any of the bear, did you?"

"Huh? The Bear? Oh, the bear! No, I didn't."

"It was because you didn't want to offend God!"

"Yes, that is so."

"Ah! So that's what makes you so different from the rest of us! You want to please God! You want to walk in…in… what's that word you once told me?"

"Integrity."

"Yes! Integrity. I suppose that was Ishpah's influence. I thought so. But in your case, no other course will serve, if you are wise."

"What do you mean?"

"Well, are you not the anointed King of Israel?" He gazed at me with warm, dark, friendly eyes, in which I saw a depth of love and commitment that made my heart leap within me. But how should I respond to this bold question? Ever since that day – you know the day I'm talking about – I had never talked about the matter with anyone. Samuel had clearly told me to be patient and to keep quiet. And so, I had; and now came this unexpected, point blank question. I answered with a question of my own.

"How many others know?"

Sol shook his head and smiled ruefully: "How many don't know! Truly, as the Lord lives, it is a secret which everyone knows. Everyone in Judah, that is. We are all waiting... waiting for the day when you will be old enough to take up arms, and take the throne, with all Judah behind you."

"That day will never come!" I assured him: "King Saul of Benjamin is the Lord's anointed, and until the day he dies, I will serve him as the Lord requires – wholeheartedly."

"But – could you not hasten the day of his death, when time and opportunity permit?"

I laughed: "What was that word we were talking about a minute ago? Integrity? Sol my father, you are a blessing to me from God, but I assure you I would rather die than raise my hand against the Lord's anointed. There is much that I do not know, but this one thing I most certainly do know. When I become king, it will be by the hand of God, not by the hand of man."

"Well," said Sol, twisting his linen cords back and forth: "What can be said? This day I have shown myself to be an unworthy fellow. A traitor to our present king, and no fit company for the future one. I am undone."

"No – you are not!" I reproved him gently: "You mean well, and are a wonderful companion, both brave and wise, and there is much that you can teach me."

"I believe," Sol interrupted solemnly, "… that it is I that will be doing the greater learning. Listen, my son David. How dare I address my future king in such a way? Listen! My son David! There is much that we can teach each other. I am honoured and blessed beyond measure to be your companion at this time. I want to serve you… and I want to serve our God… in an upright and faithful way. I bow to your judgement. May Saul live long, and well, and let God's will be done in a time of His choosing."

"You know," I mentioned, "those are almost exactly the words that Samuel used."

"Is that so? I am delighted! This godliness… this integrity… is beginning to rub off on me. David! Lend me your harp. I am going to sit on that stone over there and sing a song to the Lord."

"You are?"

"Indeed, I am! My heart is full. Maybe God will hear *me* too."

I gave Sol my harp, and sat back against the steep hillside, soothed by his heartfelt song. The distant afternoon clouds were strung across the horizon, and the sparkle of the great sea shimmered in the far distance. I was facing west towards the coastal land of the Philistines, perched high on the hill that is before Hebron. There was a reason why we had come here:

I wanted to see the gate.

What gate? you ask. Why, the town gate of Gaza, with its bars and posts, brought here on Samson's back, not fifty years ago. I was hoping for a souvenir. Fifty men could not hold up a gate such as this for a minute, and yet Samson had transported it a day's journey single-handed. Alas, there was no trace; I was fifty years too late. Maybe the men of Gaza – the Philistines – that redoubtable people from over the sea – had got it back when Samson wasn't looking, or after he had died. A town gate is not to be given up easily. There is a lot of brass, a lot of iron and a lot of wood and stone in a town gate. They are big things! – designed to keep out invading armies and to safeguard the citizens within. How demoralising it would have been to have seen Samson tear the gate out, long hair flying, empowered and invulnerable in God, and then walk off with it on his shoulders and disappear towards the hills! Well, we were here, looking to the west. I could see Gaza. I could see the sea. But the gate, I could not see.

I slept. When I awoke, Sol was next to me, and there was an hour of light left. Samson's hill was lit up by the sinking sun.

"We'll stay overnight with Caleb of Carmel," Sol told me. "The sheepfolds are an hour away, we have to hasten. Come! Let us go."

Chapter 8
An Inspiration

I slept well that night and dreamt of gates and angels. I awoke in the chill morning before the first rays of sun had lightened the sky. I slipped past the shepherds who were dozing on the last watch. I splashed my face and body with water from the nearby spring and went to higher ground to watch the new day in. It was my custom – a time of meditation and observation. In the last few weeks we had travelled steadily, Sol and I, for two reasons. One, because Sol liked to combine hunting and adventuring with shepherding – and two, because I had a fierce desire to see this land, over which I was one day to be king, so that I could know it and keep it in my heart, along with the people therein.

Travelling with Sol was like being on a permanent adventure. He knew everybody and every place, and anything he did not know he was keen to find out. The Judean hills were steep and barren on the eastern side but were productive and fruitful on the west. They ran parallel to the coast, rising at first gently then steeply from the plain to the summits. How I longed to go to the great sea! – it was only a day's travel – and paddle in the shimmering water that shone so enticingly. But alas, that was a wish that even Sol could not grant. It was enemy territory. The Philistines lived there. They lived on the coastal plain; we lived in the hills. The lines had fallen to us in pleasant places. Or so it seemed to me.

So, we wandered through hill and forest, grassland and desert; venturing a little west beyond Judah, a little north – a little east and south; always pushing the boundaries of adventure, but remaining within the borders of sense and reason. We stayed for a week in the region of Hebron during the grape harvest and admired the immense lush and vigorous vines that abounded on the stony, terraced hillsides. These grapes burst in your mouth like explosions of ecstasy. The taste and texture were divine. Their jealous owners watched over them like hawks, from outcrop and watchtower. But we placated them with goat's milk and cheese – and struck up a profitable relationship with one Heman, who lived on the outskirts of the city. He showed us favour. "May God smile on you and make straight your path before you," was his parting blessing. We were well provisioned with wine and wheat at this point and I had become acquainted with the layout of the hill country and its many towns and cities. Bethel, Ramoth, Jattir, Aroer, Siphmoth, Eshtemoa… In every fold of every hill another settlement would come into view.

It was coming into autumn, and the first of the many bird migrations would soon begin. This was a season for which Sol was prepared with his linen nets. Clouds of birds passed through the long extent of Israel twice a year. North in springtime (to I know not where) and south to Egypt and Ethiopia (wherever they may be) in autumn. When the birds passed over a certain high ridge, they would fly just above ground level, especially the quail. Sol had found this special place. It was a bare ridge that stood above the forested area near Zorah, in Dan – Samson's birthplace. The net, which was broad enough to cover a camel, was stretched on the ground between two sticks, and raised when the birds passed over. The day came. We were in position. We netted two hundred and fifty quail, and leg-tied them, alive, in bundles of five, and headed to the market of Zorah. By the end of that day, we were well provisioned indeed and had borrowed a donkey for the next few months in return for two feeble kids, which needed hand-rearing, and were not equal to the rigours of our wandering life. This donkey was a great boon. 'Badak' – Sol called it. 'Grumpy'. Sure-footed and temperamental, it carried all our stuff and was watched over by Nimrod, the dog, who formed a special attachment to it.

One morning, as I watched the sun rising into another cloudless sky and burning off the mist, I could hear the familiar sounds of the sheepfolds: the bray of our donkey, the peculiar calls of the shepherds, the scraping of rocks, the flutes, the anxious snickering of sheep waiting to be watered. Duty was calling. Far below, the tamarisk and sycamore trees on the edge of the forest were misted in dew. Within the month the small sycamore figs would begin to ripen and children would gather them from the lower branches. Sometimes we cooked the figs over a fire. What an aroma! I loved that time of year. It presaged the winter rain and cold, the months of confinement and husbandry, still a while away. Dates too were still in season. One of Sol's young daughters once asked me if I had eaten a whole bunch of dates to make my hair change colour and become shiny. It became a family joke, and they nicknamed me 'Shemesh' – the sun – which I rather liked – it helped to keep my true identity camouflaged: anonymity was a great boon.

I wandered down to the sheepfolds with the light of adventure in my eyes. In the last month or so, God had smiled on all our travels and travails. Now, we were enriched and abundant, and having travelled the length and breadth of Judah, I was keen for a truly outlandish adventure before the cold of winter drove us back to the hearths of home. Sol appeared on the path looking for me, and straight away he knew that I had something burning inside me.

"Greetings, Shemesh," he intoned with a twinkle: "What is our next assignment, O Wise One?"

I smiled at his droll comment, and for a moment thought of Joab, my troublesome brat of a cousin, who so resolutely attached himself to me and who frequently used this same odd greeting. How much freer I felt with this older, kinder man.

"I want a new adventure," I responded.

"This I can see. What is it to be?"

I gazed at him quizzically. I wanted to receive his acceptance before telling him my desire – my fixed purpose. When I could see that his heart was won – I announced winsomely, like flint in felt, yet softly and sweetly:

"We – you and I – are going to Moab."

Sol gazed at me, a mixture of emotions playing over his expressive face.

"Moab?" he echoed in disbelief; and then, with a shrug of the shoulders: "I cannot refuse."

Chapter 9
Into the Lion's Den

Why did I want to go to Moab?

I wanted to walk in the steps of our ancestors, Naomi and Ruth.

In Naomi's day – three generations ago, in the time of the Judges – all Israel was in the grip of famine, ravaged by locusts and oppressed by raiders. The country of Moab was to the east, beyond the Salt Sea. Naomi fled to Moab with her husband and her two sons (I mentioned this before…). The family settled down and in time her sons were married, but later they both died, and so did her husband. Alone and bereft and bitter in spirit, Naomi decided to return and see her days out in her hometown of Bethlehem. But what should she do about her two daughters-in-law, each of whom was childless? "Leave me, my daughters!" she wept: "You are still young. Return to your own people; marry again. Why should you come with me and bear my burden and sorrow? Surely, God's hand is heavy upon me."

One of the daughters-in-law wept and returned to her own people; the other refused to leave. Her words still ring through the ages:

"Where you go, I will go. Where you stay, I will stay. Your people will be my people, and your God will be my God. I will come with you."

This one's name was Ruth. She travelled with Naomi. They were two women, poor and homeless, and forsaken by God, on a long and difficult journey. But were they in fact forsaken by God? They accomplished the journey safely. When they reached Bethlehem, people remembered and recognised Naomi, but she no longer wished to be called Naomi, which means 'pleasant', but Mara, which means 'bitter'.

It was the time of the barley harvest. Ruth gleaned after the reapers and won favour in the eyes of a kinsman of her mother-in-law. His name was Boaz, an older man, wealthy and of good repute. He and Ruth were married – and Naomi's outlook changed once again. No longer did she call herself Mara – 'bitter'.

In time, Ruth bore a son – and great was her mother-in-law's rejoicing. The lamp of her family's line was once again burning! This was a great thing in our culture. A kinsman redeemer had been provided by God. Boaz and Ruth named their son Obed. He became the father of Jesse, who became the father of my brothers, and my sisters – and myself.

So, Ruth was my great-grandmother.

The story was frequently told and embroidered during our family times when I was young, and although I never met her, Ruth had a special place in my heart, and still does. I made enquiries about Ruth's journey and in my imagination, I had already made the trek to Moab a dozen times, going down through the Benjamin hills, skirting Jericho, crossing the River Jordan, then heading south, with the surreal cerulean of the Salt Sea on my right, picking my way through the dry, rocky, salty, barren places, until finally arriving at the cleft of the Arnon – that broad, shattered valley, with the winding river in its centre.

At last, I would arrive in my imagination at the beginning of the land of Moab, where massive mountains stood, flat-topped and separated by mighty ravines, where rain fell and dew gathered, and cattle and sheep and goats and pigs were tended by the wild Moabite people. These people – our traditional enemies, yet speaking our language and descended from Lot, Abraham's nephew – these people had taken Naomi in, and her sons and husband too. Somewhere, among the forests and ravines and mountains, was a gentle eminence on which the town of Ophar rested: the town of the people who had befriended those refugees from Israel, all those years ago. Ruth was born in this town: my great grandmother – the Moabitess.

*

Preparation for our journey was made with all speed. We returned to Bethlehem for a few days, assigned Tola, Sol's son, and Ozem, my nearest brother, to look after the sheep – and set off with Badak, our hired donkey, and Nimrod, the dog. My brothers were all home for the end of the grape harvest, and complained bitterly of favouritism and folly, that I should be permitted to go on this ridiculous journey.

It was dangerous, unnecessary and stupid – and so was I. This was Eliab's analysis of the situation. He had a short way with words and never minced them. I would have dearly liked to have repaid him in kind, but I kept my eye on the prize and pretended indifference. This actually infuriated him even more, so I was inwardly rejoicing. I liked getting my own way, especially against opposition, and I usually did. My father, who for some reason gave me his approval, nonetheless seemed troubled and took an age to bless us and let us go on our way. As we departed, I turned and was shocked to see a common look in the eyes of those who watched us go: they believed we weren't coming back. My father looked old and gaunt. I hesitated.

"We don't have to go," Sol murmured.

I smiled and tossed my head cheerfully: "We are going! God is with us! If Ruth could do it, we can."

"David!" It was Zeruiah, my sister. "David: rub charcoal in your hair and on your face. You look too young and fine, a target for thieves and brigands. Come here! Take this. Leave the harp – you will be back in a few days. Take care."

She pressed a knife into my hands. It was steel, not bronze, in a leather sheath. I recognised it: it was a prized possession – her husband's – no one was allowed to touch it. She gave me a look of fire that communicated itself to me and quenched that spirit of uncertainty that was beginning to rise.

"I'll have it back when you return," she hissed.

"That Zeruiah is a fine spitting cobra," Sol informed me, as we headed for the hills. I chuckled. It was an apt description, not that I had seen too many spitting cobras – only one in fact, and that at a safe distance. It was brought from beyond the vast desert on a boat from distant lands and traded for by the nomads.

"I miss my harp."

"Her sons are fine boys," Sol observed: "I expect great things of them. Fine boys they are."

We trekked on in silence, making good speed since we had no sheep to worry about. I reflected on Abishai and Joab, the fine boys: the future mighty men of Judah. With a mother like Zeruiah, how could they be anything but? And Asahel too, of course. He might even be greater than them both. But they were such a handful, especially the first two. I looked gratefully at Sol's strong back as he stepped firmly up the rocky path in front of me, leading the donkey. How grateful I was to have someone strong and faithful and caring – and easy-going. I lifted my eyes to the Lord of the late afternoon sky, and my spirit lifted within me. This was going to be an adventure!

*

Bethlehem is in the hills, a day's journey from the Jordan River, providing you start early. It was via the Jordan that I wished to travel – boyishly indifferent to the advice of those who knew better. I wanted to cross this historic river to the south of Jericho, close to where it entered the Salt Sea. Sol, who knew better, put up no objection. We left late – at midday – and kept to the paths less travelled. At the highest point we could glimpse Mount Nebo in the east and the Great Sea in the west. The Salt Sea was still concealed from view by the intervening hills. This was the same route I had taken a year before with the Bethlehem Boys, the day we were victors over the Benjamin Bullies. There was no love lost between Benjamin and Judah, and it was partly their territory we had to pass through on our way to the Jordan. We planned to skirt around the edge of the Sea, where the land is rocky and bare. That way we were less likely to meet anyone. The Jericho

Road was not for us. It descended through the barren desert ravines and was the haunt of robbers: we kept to the heights. As the afternoon wore on, we reached the point where the steep descent from the hills begins. The descent seems endless. Far below, in the distance, the Jordan valley was divided by a ribbon of green, dense jungle where the river flowed – and from where we stood, we could see the Plains of Moab beyond, broad and flat and brown, and beyond them in the distance – Mount Nebo. On our right, the mountains were bare and arid, as they descended towards the Dead Sea. On our left, to the west, tongues of forest crept up the gullies from the lower country and then gave way to grass and scrub and rock. Nimrod plunged down a gully after a young deer – and disappeared among the trees. As I saw him go, a strange feeling crept over me – it was a sense of isolation, and of menace.

*

We continued on for a while then stopped and waited for my dog to catch up with us. Normally he would have re-joined us by now. We waited until dark. Nimrod did not reappear. In the distance we saw a fire flicker.

"Hold the donkey, Shemesh," Sol whispered: "Wait here. I will go ahead and see who it is. Hopefully they are shepherds and we can stay with them tonight."

He turned to go then hesitated and turned back to me: "Use the charcoal. Let us not take any risks. If anyone wishes to know – you are my son." The whites of his eyes flashed in the darkness, and I detected a look of… well… apprehension, to say the least. Why is it, I wondered, that we are both suddenly fearful? This has never happened before.

I decided to take notice. I tethered the donkey to a rock and then ground up the charcoal – our kindling – into fine powder in our wooden kneading trough. I damped my hands and ran the charcoal powder through my hair, and over my face and arms and legs. I rolled on the ground in the dust and dirt. Sheep droppings clung to my cloak. In the meantime, rough voices were raised in anger over at the fire. What could be going on?

Sol needed me.

My heart sank when I saw the situation. A group of men – shepherds indeed and not bandits – were gathered around my companion with clubs at the ready. Sol was on his haunches, defensively, hands spread, unarmed, talking and talking… persuading… trying to keep them at bay. Instantaneously I recognised three of the group and in the same instant I threw myself into their midst, crying out incoherently like a mad creature, and cast myself upon Sol, making grunts and screams and whimpers. My arrival in this lunatic fashion dispelled all immediate threats of violence. The men stood back in aversion and contempt. I nestled into Sol fiercely, trembling violently, with my lower lip sticking out and my eyes staring. I would have slobbered for greater effect if my mouth had not been so dry.

"Shemesh! Shemesh!" Sol uttered soothingly, holding me to him like a baby.

"So – this is he? This is your son, whom you are travelling with?" rasped a surly shepherd. "Why did you not tell us he was demon possessed? Go! Get out of here! Begone, back to

Judah, where you belong! If we see you again, we will feed your carcasses to the vultures."

A volley of stones and curses followed us as we fled back the way we had come. As we left, I shrieked and staggered towards one of the men. He stepped back hastily. These were crude but superstitious men, and demonic possession they wanted nothing to do with. Who could blame them? Sol grabbed me roughly and dragged me gibbering into the night. It wasn't until we were at a safe distance that the rocks and curses came. I kept up the gibbering and shrieking all the way back to the donkey, then subsided into whimpering and eventually silence, as we hastened away.

*

Later that night, the moon came up, and, peering over a cliff edge, we saw the Salt Sea laid out far below us. The next morning found us on its empty shores. All night we had kept walking, putting as much distance as possible between ourselves and the brutes of Benjamin. Finally, we paused for a halt. Badak licked at the salt and looked around for Nimrod.

"We've lost Nimrod!" I stated.

"We have indeed, and that is the Lord's doing. We would never have got out alive with your dog there to identify you."

This was true. One of the shepherds was Cush. The dreaded Cush. He knew me by the dog, and my disguise would not have availed if Nimrod had appeared. My pretence at being Sol's son would have come under scrutiny then.

"What happened to him, do you think?"

"Leopard. Or wolf. I saw signs of leopard in that valley. The dog won't be coming back. He served you well. Never better than last night."

I nodded. I felt tired, hungry, thirsty, insecure and vulnerable, but – alive: and this was no place to stay for long. "I'm hungry," I mentioned. "What shall we do?"

"Our best course is to go on to the Plain of the Jordan, where we can find shelter and water and hiding. To go back the way we have come is to risk encountering those ruffians again."

"I agree. How long will it take?"

"Six hours, maybe. We will have to husband our water supply and just keep going. Here, chew on this." He gave me a hard biscuit and some dried goat meat and a piece of cheese. It was tough on the jaws but my body assimilated it as if it was nectar, and my eyes brightened.

As we walked, alone and insignificant, along the radiant beach, that sense of being in God's protecting hand returned. We discussed last night's events:

"They were going to kill us," Sol asserted solemnly. "That was the very reason for their gathering. You are no longer safe being a shepherd. Cush does not know – but he suspects – that you are the one who will take over Saul's throne, and he has set out to kill you. And he is a man mighty in battle, before whom few can stand… and we walked right into his camp."

"So – what did you say when you saw them? What did they say to you?"

Sol shook his head reflectively: "I greeted them in the customary way – 'Peace be to you, my brothers' – and immediately was set upon by Cush, who declared I was a spy travelling with the son of Jesse, and that God had delivered us into their hands. All of them stood over me and accused and threatened."

"I heard the shouts. And how did you respond? What did you say?"

"I'm travelling with my son, Shemesh. We are searching for two lost goats. To keep their interest, I began describing how we lost the goats and where, but they did not believe me. They were convinced that you were with me. We would have been killed if you had not come to the rescue. Well – I would, anyway. Whatever made you think of that idea, pretending to be mad? That was – that was… that was ridiculous! But – it was brilliant!"

"Well – it worked," I said, soberly: "Did you by any chance notice their faces towards the end? They were more frightened than we were!"

Sol gave me a sidelong glance and smiled and shook his head. He began to laugh. I began to laugh. Before long we were laughing so hard, we had to stop and slap our sides. Badak looked on scornfully.

"You were so convincing!" Sol spluttered: "I actually thought you were really my son, and really mad as well."

"That's what acting is all about, isn't it?" I responded: "It's being the part… actually becoming the person you are pretending to be. Believe me, I was acting for my life. I was extremely frightened."

Sol nodded.

We walked on in silence. Then a thought came to him, strongly: "Listen, David. We are embarking on a journey we cannot turn back from. Should we not commit each and every day, and every decision to the Lord in prayer?"

I nodded: "Let us do so then."

"Just wait a moment," Sol added thoughtfully. "We need to have a sacrifice, don't we, or an offering, surely?"

"I don't think God will require us to do so in our situation. It is our hearts that he is looking on. That's what we are offering."

A strange look passed across my companion's face, as when mist lifts from the mountains. "Very well then: let us pray as we are," he agreed. And so – we did – on that and every other day that we journeyed together.

Chapter 10
On the Shores of Time

We reached the mouth of the Jordan River around midday, and followed its barren shore north, leaving the Salt Sea behind us. This was not our direction, but our eyes were sore from the salty glare, our feet were burning, and we craved coolness and shade. We found it eventually, upstream, and cooled off in the water and laid down in a grove of palm trees. This was my first date palm grove, and a few late clusters had been overlooked. My slingshot brought down a couple. Oh, joy! Dates!

We slept for some hours fitfully, then packed ourselves up, and went on our way in the late afternoon. I would like to have said 'in the cool of the late afternoon', but cool was a word that seldom came to mind when walking in the Jordan Valley. It was very warm. How I missed the mountains of Judah. Nonetheless, crossing the Jordan was for both of us a spiritual experience. This river, so crucial in the life and history of our nation, was a reminder of God's covenant with us, his people.

I had heard the Jordan spoken of all my life and now here I was – actually in it! The river was slow and clear and full-bodied and – it was actually cool. Where, I wondered, did so much water come from when it hadn't rained for months? Sol could not answer this question so we just accepted it as a mystery, and, crossing over where we could, reached the Plains of Moab, and headed south.

The Plains of Moab, so called, were not in Moab. That country was a day's march away. The plains were a broad, flat area where Moses had gathered the children of Israel – our nation – before Joshua led them across the Jordan. God held the river back and the people crossed on dry land – three million of them. This was at a point near Gilgal, a town further upstream and closer to Jericho. I would have loved to have made the short pilgrimage to Gilgal from where we were – but resisted the temptation out of a sense of caution – another new experience for me. I did not want to walk into any more hornets' nests…

So… where was I? Moses… and then… Joshua.

Joshua went into the Promised Land, but Moses never did. He saw it from the top of Mount Nebo, which is where God had told him to go – and then – he died – and no man knows his body's final resting place. But Yahweh does. He knows all things.

Yahweh is a name for our God. I like it a lot. It sounds spacious and vast and all-encompassing – like breath. Yah-weh…

'God' sounds rather short and business-like – and not so grand and mysterious as I'd like it to be. 'Yahweh' fills me with yearning and wonder. It's so poetic. Well… ah… so… Moses died, Joshua crossed the river… and I would have liked to have gone to Gilgal and I would have liked to have climbed Mount Nebo – but these were temptations I resisted.

"Oh Lord, let me keep my eyes on where I am going, and not get drawn away by distractions, no matter how sweet or enticing." That was a prayer that came to me that day and it was just right for our journey. I know Ishpah would have approved of it – and Joseph, and Ruth, and Michael.

*

Well, I decided that the dishevelled look was prudent for me in these strange places, and I was very careful to play the part of a simple son to Sol. I kept my hair tousled and dirty, along with my face and clothes, and said little to the people we met. And the little I did say made little sense. We were now in the land of Gad and Reuben, our fellow Israelites. Their land lay to the east of the Jordan and the Salt Sea. The people we met were friendly, hospitable, curious and courteous – however, our journey quickly led us away from the inhabited areas. By nightfall we were walking parallel with the Salt Sea, sometimes a little inland, sometimes along the actual shore, depending on the terrain. It was rough going, and smelly. There were yellow stains on the rocks, from sulphur, and large cakes of bitumen dotted the shoreline. I poked them with my staff. The path was non-existent and we had to pick our way through the maze of glistening gullies and salt-stacks and cliffs. We stopped for a few hours to rest and refresh and when the moon came up in the east, we commenced walking again. That moonrise was lovely. The mountains of Judah were black silhouettes. The sea glistened. The sky sparkled. And it was cool! We continued south, picking our way with care while the moon made its stately procession across the sky.

"When I see the moon and the stars, which you have created, what is Man that you are mindful of Him?" I asked the Eternal One.

"Fine words for a simpleton!" Sol commented, but his tone belied his words. We felt both humbled and uplifted by the power of God's creation around us. We were drawn together in shared wonder. We were kindred spirits… travellers on the shores of time… watchers in the night…

The moon set over the hills to the east and we rested until dawn. Then – some water, some dried figs, some fresh dates, and we continued along the shore. At times we had to backtrack when the cliffs stood into the water. Our progress was slow but steady. They were magnificent, those bleached, towering cliffs, honeycombed with caves – but nothing prepared us for the sight of the gorge of the Arnon, where the River Arnon runs into the Salt Sea. This was the northern boundary of Moab. We had arrived! … sort of…

The gorge was stupendous. I had expected a broad shattered valley with a shallow, stony ribbon of water issuing forth, up which we could easily travel. What we found was a meandering procession of deep, tranquil pools, each like massive stairs, with sluices and great waterfalls in polished rock. This idyllic sight, like nothing I had ever seen or imagined before, was crouched at the foot of towering pink walls of smooth rock, that swooped up to the very sky, so high that the only sky we could see was a thin ribbon of blue, and at the foot of the gorge all was shadow, except for a few rays of sun that bounced and refracted on the water pools.

Sol removed his sturdy sandals and stood at the edge of a shallow pool, gazing at this spectacle with awe and concern. At length he shook his head:

"We won't get the donkey up there!" he stated. He grinned. It was time for our midday rest, and what better place than this! Water, shade, tranquillity, complete isolation; we could even have a fire.

When I awoke it was mid-afternoon. Sol was asleep. Badak stood disconsolate at his tether. A brilliant bird landed on the tether for a moment then sped up the canyon like a blue flash. My boyish heart hungered to see how far up the gorge I could get and what wonders it would reveal. So, I took off my sandals and set off, every sense highly tuned. How awe-inspiring this exploration turned out to be! I walked beside still waters, I climbed up falls, I skirted waterspouts, all alone – amidst the silent majesty of the sweeping pink and yellow polished walls that reached up to the sky. After many twists and turns, I came to a waterfall that was impassable. It flowed into a deep, clear, capacious pool, in which tiny fish hung, suspended. Tussocks of grass clung on here and there, and out of a crack in the wall sprang tiny blue flowers. There were caves too, which I passed with trepidation – Zeruiah's steel knife glinting in my hand. Leopards? Bears? Surely not. What would they live on? The obvious answer in this case was… me… But… there were none.

I took up my station on a smooth rock at the water's edge, with my feet dangling in the pool, and cast my eyes all around, absorbing the feeling of this place. It was a temple, a tabernacle, a monument unto the Lord. Unstained by the blood of sacrifice and the minds of men. The bird sped past me with a fish wriggling in its beak. A ray of afternoon sun caught its wing for a moment, and again that flash of blue captured my sight. It flew over the impassable waterfall like a thought, no doubt on its way to its young ones, perched in a cleft higher up. I sat scanning the walls and noticed a small rock sitting high on a ledge. Time for some target practice! My sling-stone missed its target and ricocheted off first one wall and then the other. As it did so, the crack of the impact split the silence and echoes ran up and down the chamber like goats leaping from rock to rock. My eyes lit up with delight! I spotted where my stone fell and went to retrieve it, uttering high-pitched shepherd cries – some staccato, some drawn out. The gorge filled up with sounds that first swelled then subsided, like waves rushing back and forth. I raised my voice in melodic calls and in the songs of my people, and the great canyon accompanied me and sang back to me.

When I returned to our camp Sol was standing by Badak, packed and ready.

"Time to go," he announced, gently.

"No!" I protested. "First, you must walk where I have walked, and see for yourself what wonders there are to be seen!"

He shook his head and gave me a fatherly smile.

"I have seen them already," he told me. "They are written on your face. I do not need to see more. Come. We need to find grazing for our cantankerous friend. The hour is getting late."

IN THE VALLEY OF THE JORDAN.

Chapter 11
Two Meetings

We had a pretty good idea of the geography of Moab. Often had I studied this land from the vantage point of the Judean hills, above the springs of En Gedi. It was in fact only a morning's saunter from En Gedi, in Judah, to the mighty gorge of the Arnon River in Moab. But – there was an obstacle: the Salt Sea. If we had had a boat we could have paddled across in an hour or two, but Bethlehem was not noted for boat builders. It was hikers that our town specialised in – we were good at that. And anyway, how would we get a boat from our village to the Salt Sea? It was a long and difficult descent. Samson would have managed it. He would have ploughed across the sea on foot, quite possibly – it is, after all, impossible to sink in the Salt Sea.

My friend Michael: dear little Michael – now a servant to Saul these past few months – had a great idea for getting across the sea: fill some wineskins with air, strap them to your feet, and walk across. I believe it would have worked. I wouldn't like to be stuck in the middle of the sea if something went wrong, though.

As I said before, we had studied the geography of Moab from afar, and roughly knew what to expect. Big rugged steep hills – split by massive canyons – that was it. And we knew enough not to go walking too far up the stony, arid canyons looking for pasture and habitation. It was on higher areas – the mountain plateaus and edges that we would find this. Accordingly, we went south looking for a way to the hilltops. In time a ravine split the impregnable, towering cliffs and we followed it inland, keeping a sharp eye out for a path to the plateau; and we found one. It was more of a goat's track than a highway, but it conducted us safely above the cliffs and then we were walking around a gentle, forested, mountain shoulder. We could smell smoke and sense habitation. Any moment now… we were going to meet our first Moabite.

"How do you feel?" Sol asked.

"Ah, nervous… how do you feel?"

"Like a sitting duck."

We were just debating whether to camp for the night, since dusk was gathering, when a man appeared out of the forest heading in our direction. He was wearing a cloak and head-dress, unlike our own, and was unaware of our presence. He carried a bulging bag and bow and arrows. We stood there, in an unthreatening pose, waiting for him to notice us. He did so, but not until almost upon us, and then started violently and came to an abrupt halt. Reassured by our un-hostile demeanour, he studied us with sharp, watchful eyes.

"Greetings, travellers, where are you from?" he asked in strange accents.

Sol was our spokesman. I was his simple son, with tousled, charcoaled hair, and downcast gaze and slack shoulders.

"Greetings, O mighty hunter of the forest," Sol responded. "We are travellers indeed, from across the Sea of Salt, from Bethlehem in Judah. I am Sol, son of Pisgah, this is Shemesh, my son. We are your servants."

He bowed, nudging me to follow suit, and then straightened up again. "Pray, accept this gift as a token of our good will, if it pleases you."

Sol offered our stranger a cake of figs, which he had stowed at the top of our baggage in preparation for such an occasion as this. I watched tensely to see how this gift would be received. I was not tense for long.

"I am Atto ben Hadad, son of Herash. Peace be with you, and the blessings of the mighty ones be upon you. I receive your gift with gratitude. Pray, stay with me tonight. You have travelled far and are weary. I entreat you to accept my hospitality, humble as it is, and wash your feet in comfort and in peace."

"Thank you, my father." Sol responded, bowing once more, myself copying his actions. "We are in your debt. We humbly accept your kindness. It is a great blessing to us."

A look, a smile, a hug, and now – no longer was the hunter a stranger. Now he was our host and provider. Our guardian. Our passport. Our friend.

It was dark when we reached Atto ben Hadad's home. At dawn a sweet aroma wafted in from the clay oven that was outside. Atto's wife was making flatbread from rye flour. We ate the bread with curds of goat's milk, and our host offered us his services as our guide. He knew the mountains of Moab intimately.

"But how can we repay him?" I asked Sol in private. The opportunity was God-given, and we wanted to take it, but what had we to offer in return?

"My hunting net?" Sol suggested: "Your knife?"

I shook my head. "I cannot. It is not mine to give."

"Then… then we cannot. We will ask him for directions and continue on our way. Maybe it is better so."

We approached our host and thanked him for his hospitality and declined his kind offer to be our guide (I had dropped my pretence of simpleness by this time). We explained that we were poor men, travelling lightly, and had no way of repaying him. To our great surprise he overruled our objections and with humble dignity requested the privilege of being our guide, nonetheless, requiring no other payment than that privilege. This was indeed a welcome turn of events and our spirits rose. We accepted and began chatting enthusiastically together. How far? How long? What type of country? Where is Ophar?

"The village you are looking for is south of Kir Hareseth. Two days hence. We must go inland over the mountains, then follow the King's Highway south towards Edom. Ophar is near there. Listen to me my brothers: it is not good for you to be dressed in this way; you look like Hebrews. I will give each of you a tribal head-dress, such as is worn both in Moab and in Edom. In this way we will attract less attention and you will travel more safely through these wild places. Would this please you?"

This pleased us very well.

The ascent to the highlands of Moab was long and arduous. The tracks ran from one habitation to the next, each little hamlet clinging to a precarious living and peopled by dark-eyed, swarthy, wary tribes-people – much like ourselves. It was the resting hour. We stopped for our midday rest under a terebinth tree and attended to our various bodily needs. Badak, unencumbered by his load and loosely tethered, grazed contentedly on the rough grass and sedges in the nearby gully. When I awoke there was no sign of him. My heart sank. First Nimrod, whom I missed dearly, but he had served me well in his parting, and now Badak, without whom we could not do.

I grabbed the tether rope and ran down the gully. After turning a couple of corners, there he was! But not alone… another group of travellers was having a midday rest: they were investigating the finer points of their new donkey. I came to a halt and greeted them silently with a bow. Atto had forbidden me to talk; my accent gave me away. I held up the tether in a mute signal of ownership and watched distress, disappointment and resignation pass across their faces. Their free donkey – that happy dream – so soon to be taken away. But there was one face there that did not register these emotions; and on this face, curiosity and attraction was written. It was a girl; unveiled. Her mother quickly turned the girl around, but the look stayed with me. It was young. It was fresh. It was enchanting. It made me quiver. That night my dreams and inner desires came together in a flood. Waking up was disorienting.

Notwithstanding my inner longings… distance and new horizons soon separated me from this chance encounter. I regained my composure and my purpose and was able to focus on the journey at hand. And this was just as well…

The King's Highway was the main thoroughfare for traders and travellers of all descriptions. It wound through the high hilltops and plateaus of Moab, skirting the ends of the deep chasms that spiked liked crooked teeth from the edge of the Salt Sea. The highway ran all the way from Egypt to the unknown north.

Where there were travellers, there were robbers. One day we came across a lone youth, bludgeoned to death off the track, robbed of whatever was his. We kept our clubs and weapons of war at the ready – and proceeded at high alert. It was a relief to join up with another larger group of travellers. They too, were glad to be strengthened in number. We reached Kir Hareseth at the end of the second day and, thanks to our guide, were permitted entry to the city. The gates were closed behind us.

*

Moabites worshipped Baal, the god of fertility – among other gods – and we had arrived on a significant day of worship and sacrifice. All the locals were there.

That night we found ourselves witnessing a ritual from the rooftop where we had found lodging. The altar stood on a built-up courtyard of stone, which was lit up by torchbearers and flaming pots. The smell of pitch and oil was strong. Incantations, invocations, dancing, swaying; the scene was absorbing and mesmerising. A premonition of impending frenzy alarmed me. I was glad to be on the roof; anonymous, invisible, unseen. I was used to sacrifices – it was part of our religion and culture, but this was beyond my experience. There seemed to be something dark and dreadful lurking behind the scenes. And what was going on in the background? Those painted eyes; that gleaming hair; that flash of silver. Was it what I thought it was? I was not comfortable, and as the evening wore on, my comfort grew less.

In the morning I talked to Atto ben Hadad. We had become close, like father and son, and I trusted him.

"I am used to sacrifices," I explained, "but not human ones."

He shook his head as if reluctant to disagree with me.

"What we desire from our gods is the very best," he explained. "Wine, wheat, flesh, fruit, health, life, protection; all these things. To get the very best we must also give it. What is more precious than human life?"

It was my turn to shake my head. I hesitated to say what was in my heart, but it would not be pent up:

"There is but one God! The God of Israel: Yahweh. He alone is worthy of our praise and worship, and he does not desire the blood of men. It is loathsome to him. This Baal is a false god. Evil – and…" my words failed me.

Atto gazed at me with compassion and a degree of respect. "David, my son… (I had disclosed to him my true identity and the nature of my quest) – David, my son: I hear what you are saying and with all my heart – I believe you… It must have been your God that brought us together… and for your sake I would choose to serve him – but… I am not a Hebrew…"

I was silent for a short while, then responded:

"Thank you, my father, for your understanding. Truly it is God's doing that you have taken us into your care. You are like bread and wine to us."

We embraced.

Our guide was a respected man and known to Cushan, the King of Moab. I was with him when the king entered the marketplace.

"Is this not a Hebrew?" Cushan demanded, studying my sandals.

"Yes, my lord," Atto replied. "He is David, son of Jesse of Bethlehem. He is travelling with me in search of his relatives in the village of Ophar."

"Ahhh…" the elderly king puffed, addressing me: "You must be related to Ruth, who went to Bethlehem with a Hebrew woman many years ago. Is this so?"

"It is so, my lord."

I bowed, abandoning my pretence of backwardness. "I am her great grandson. How do you know of my great grandmother?"

"That is a long story," the king chuckled. "It was before my time, of course, but only just. Come. Sit with me and let us talk. We can exchange stories. I am interested in such matters."

I spent the morning in the company of Cushan, King of Moab. By the time our ways parted, I had made an unexpected friend. Later in the morning Sol joined us. He had taken part in the festivities and drunk deeply of the wine of dissipation. The lapis stone that had adorned his staff was missing – and I guessed why. In part I envied him and in part I despised him. Nonetheless, I was curious as to his experiences in that realm of the flesh that was as yet a mystery to me. I sounded him out as we continued our journey. We had so far spent four nights on our quest, and here we were, in another world, and close to our destination. I went straight to the point.

"Was she fair of face, this woman of Moab?"

His face fell. "I regret…" he began, "but… what is done is done. I was carried away by wine and perfume and desire – and today I am the worse for it. I have fallen in your esteem once again, and in my own." He gazed at me mournfully.

"And? Was she fair of face?" I repeated.

He shrugged: "It's possible. I will never know since she was wearing a veil. I like to think so – but let us not continue along this line. We live, we make mistakes, we learn from them."

Atto chuckled.

Eventually, the rough track – the King's Highway as it is called – swooped up to an outlook from which we could see the mountains continuing south to Edom. Lower down, on a small ridge with terraced gardens above and below, an un-walled village perched. Our guide spread out an expressive hand:

"Ophar!" he announced with satisfaction. "The home of your ancestor."

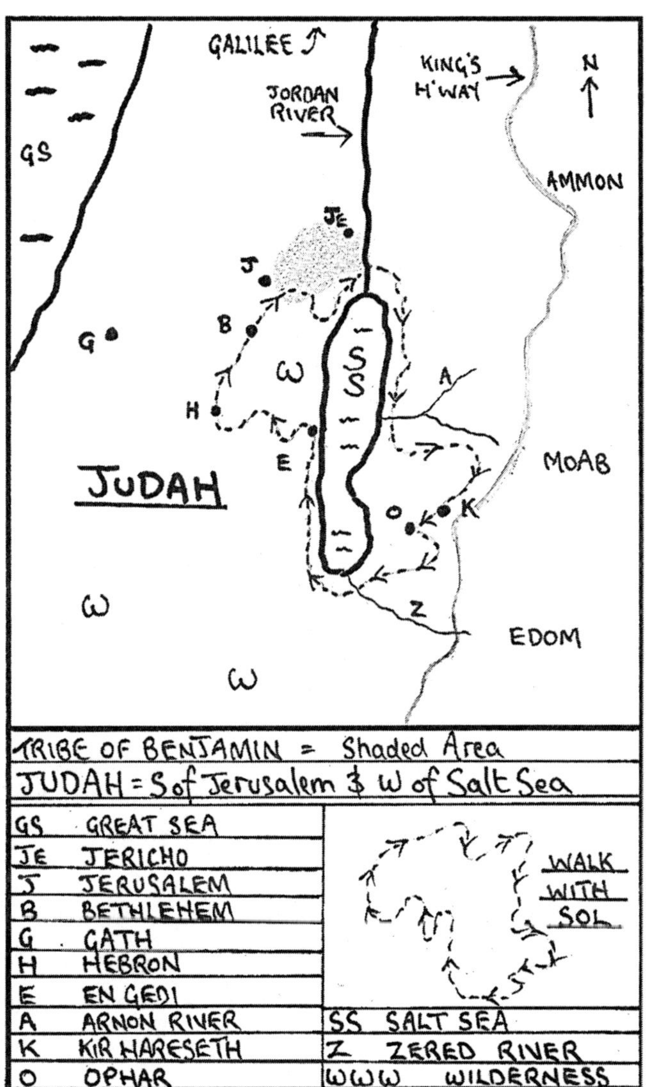

GALILEE
JORDAN RIVER
KING'S H'WAY
N
AMMON
GS
JE
J
G
B
W
H
E
A
MOAB
O
K
Z
EDOM
JUDAH
W
W
WALK WITH SOL
TRIBE OF BENJAMIN = Shaded Area
JUDAH = S of Jerusalem & W of Salt Sea
GS   GREAT SEA
JE   JERICHO
J   JERUSALEM
B   BETHLEHEM
G   GATH
H   HEBRON
E   EN GEDI
A   ARNON RIVER
K   KIR HARESETH
O   OPHAR
SS   SALT SEA
Z   ZERED RIVER
WWW   WILDERNESS

Chapter 12
Reflections

We arrived back in Bethlehem in the resting hour. There were few to see us and little interest was shown. Nine nights had passed since we set off on our journey. Sol bade me farewell and went to his home, taking Badak with him. I looked around hopefully. Would Nimrod detach himself from the undergrowth and come loping towards me, light of foot, intelligent of face, and affectionate? Alas, it was not to be. The only dogs to be seen were the slinking curs that hung around the edge of town – yellow, lean, and ugly. My faithful friend was no more.

I went to Zeruiah's home. She was resting on the roof under a shelter of branches. I sprang up the rough outer stairs and she greeted me warmly:

"You have travelled far and you have returned. May the Lord be praised! But I never feared for your safety. Quickly! Go and present yourself to our father. He is weary with worry, like Jacob over Joseph, wondering will you return. But first, you may return my knife. Thank-you. Has it seen much service? Only in hunting? That is good. No… you may keep it… And was your pilgrimage successful?"

"Indeed."

"Let us listen to the account this evening after dinner. The family will meet at our father's home to celebrate your return. I will see to it. I will also invite Sol and his family."

*

That evening, after dinner, my family heard the account of our pilgrimage to Moab. I omitted a certain sensitive part, but otherwise was quite detailed in my story. It was the tradition in our tribe to listen to stories, but it was unusual for the youngest member of the family to be doing the telling. My father, however, was proud and enthusiastic, so I gave full rein to my descriptive powers and presented as glowing a picture as I could of our adventures.

Because Sol was there, Eliab – my disapproving elder brother – bottled up his resentment and in time actually grew interested himself. It was a memorable evening. The bonds of family, often stretched by rivalry and resentment, were renewed and strengthened. There was a sense of stepping back into the time of Ruth and Naomi as the story unfolded – and we each had a feeling of being part of that story… and of new stories yet to be.

*

Our time in Ophar had been sweet. Ruth's family still lived there, and after we had made enquiries and explained ourselves, her present-day relatives were eager to find out what had happened to her. Her departure to Israel was an event which was still remembered and talked about. After she left, nothing more was heard of her. Now, generations later, a blood relative of their long-gone ancestor appeared out of the blue, with the answers to this mystery. These people were my relatives too, and they received us warmly.

When we arrived in Ophar I was eager to get the charcoal out of my hair and face and the dirt out of my cloak and tunic. On our first night a mighty thunderstorm crashed over our heads. It was like the voice of God: lightning split the sky and rain came down in torrents. I found a flat, grassy spot away from the homes and stripped off and washed thoroughly, rejoicing in the fury of the elements. What a welcome home! In the morning I was a different person – chestnut hair, shining eyes, glowing face, clean garments. Our hosts hardly recognised me.

Atto ben Hadad stayed with us for the two days we were there and went hunting for deer early one morning. He came back with a pig instead, and a banquet was prepared in our honour, with music, dancing, story-telling and pantomime. The villagers gathered on the threshing floor for the occasion and wine flowed. Sol looked at the pig meat simmering in the large copper pot and gazed at me sidelong.

"What do we do in this situation? We can't eat pig!" he muttered, spreading his hands in confusion. Atto cocked his head towards us to catch my whispered reply. He understood our predicament.

"Just pretend it's bear," I advised, cheekily, "and watch out for the wine. We are honoured guests, don't forget."

Atto chuckled.

*

The next morning, he took us up to the highway and showed us our way back home: first we would travel via the hills of Edom and then head across the Arabah, which was the flat expanse of land below the southern tip of the Salt Sea. I gave him a present: it was written on a piece of goatskin. I read it out for him:

"Give to the Lord O you sons of the mighty,
Give to the Lord – glory and strength.
Give to the Lord the glory due his name;
Worship the Lord in the beauty of holiness.
The voice of the Lord is over the waters,
The God of glory thunders.
The voice of the Lord is powerful;
The voice of the Lord is full of majesty.
The voice of the Lord breaks the cedars –
Yea – it splinters the cedars of Lebanon.
He makes them also skip like a calf:
Lebanon and Sirion like a young wild ox.
The voice of the Lord divides flames of fire,
The voice of the Lord shakes the wilderness,
The voice of the Lord shakes the wilderness of Kadesh.
The voice of the Lord makes the deer give birth.
And strips the forests bare –
And in his temple every voice cries: "Glory!"
The Lord sits enthroned over the flood,
The Lord is enthroned as king forever.
The Lord gives strength to his people,
The Lord blesses his people – with peace."
(I had written this psalm the day after the thunderstorm.)

"I will cherish this gift, as from one heart to another," Atto, our benefactor, assured us simply: "Even though I do not read, one day my children will read this to me again. May the God of Glory watch over you and make your path straight and true."

We embraced and went our opposite ways.

Sol shrugged expressively. "God is watching over you like an eagle over its chick, David my son. He has brought fortune and favour to shine upon you! This man, this hunter, is he not an angel sent from heaven? He is worthy to have my hunter's net. I am glad it is in his keeping. When he catches a pig in its folds, he will think of me."

We hurried along the edge of the land of Edom, our ancient enemy, clad in grubby apparel – tousled and dirty, wearing our Moabite head-dresses and speaking to no one. After a half-day's journey, we reached the Arabah, that desolate, flat wasteland that borders the Salt Sea and the Jordan River. There we encountered ruffians, even wilder and dirtier than ourselves, and equally unwilling to speak. They were salt cutters and mud hawkers. Can you imagine selling mud? But all kinds of odd health and beauty stuff found a market in the far-off homes and citadels of the rich and powerful.

In Kir Hareseth, for example, the indulgence of the Moabite king was legendary. Cushan had sixty wives and a hundred concubines. That's a lot of mud baths. Our own king – King Saul – had only one wife and one or two concubines. He was far too busy repelling our enemies to spare any thought for beauty treatments. Nonetheless, he did have a court, and courtiers, and attendants in Gibeah – and Michael, my little friend, was one of his attendants. What must that be like, I wondered? How was Michael faring?

It was a long and arduous journey. We went across the Arabah then followed the track next to the Salt Sea to En Gedi, then climbed the cliffs and trudged up through the wilderness of Judah and returned home via Hebron.

Long and arduous it was. But it was the traditional route… and only half as tough as the way we had come. All those wise advisors whom I had ignored at the outset of our journey… they were right. This is the way Naomi and Ruth would actually have come, all those years ago, I now believed. We camped at the springs of En Gedi on the first night and stayed with Heman of Hebron on the second – our final night of the journey. Our Moabite head-dresses were packed away now, and we looked and felt more like ourselves. We had found friends and favour in the land of Moab, this despite the many battles, some quite recent, that our nations had fought against each other. When, I wondered, would we enjoy their favour again?

*

A few days after our return the new moon appeared. Beacons were lit on hilltops and trumpets were blown. The Feast of Tabernacles was about to begin – in thanksgiving for the past year's crops – and as a reminder that our forefathers had lived in tents in the wilderness (a tabernacle was another name for a tent – or shelter). Winter was fast approaching, the harvesting was all done – and the days were bright and cool. The festival took place over eight days, and lambs, rams, kids, bullocks, calves and goats would be sacrificed. There would be storytelling, dancing, pantomime, music and sacred rituals; also, prayer and the reading of the law; and – banquets and games.

Suddenly I was a boy again – my last Arabian summer of boyhood. Off to the outskirts of the forest we went with axes and machetes to gather branches for the huts. These huts – or tabernacles – were to be our shelters for the eight days of the festival. Later they would be taken down and used for home repairs and for firewood for the winter. We gathered willow and poplar and oak and acacia… carob, terebinth and tamarisk. We avoided the sycamore fig – it oozed sticky, white sap – and back to the encampment we went, time and again, while the fathers and older sons constructed and tied up the rough shelters.

The women were busy, of course, ferrying water and provisions, and standing guard over what was theirs, and talking and feeding babies. Young children ran around excitedly, or looked on with big, dark eyes at this scene of activity… or played games… or explored. Pipes were played, harps and lyres stroked, tambourines and drums shaken and tapped.

'Three times a year shall all your males present themselves to the Lord' decreed our law.

This, the third and final festival, was the most relaxed and joyful. The harvesting was all over for another year: ahead lay the winter months, when rain would water the earth, and snow might blanket the brown land, and ploughing and sowing and maintenance would be done. Then, from out of its wintry grip, the land would rise, green and flowering, to greet a new year, and seeding, weeding, pruning and watering – it would all begin again.

I went down to the edge of the forest with Abishai and the boys and we hung perilously from trees as we cut our branches. There were no low branches – they had all been taken in previous years. Sol passed by with Badak and his young sons to gather branches from deeper in the forest, where they were lower. He tapped his head expressively when he saw us up in the canopy. His sons waved to me excitedly.

"Hi Shemesh!" they called.

Joab looked at me inquisitively: "Shemesh? Is that what they call you?"

"I'll explain later if you like," I offered with a grin.

"If it pleases you," he accepted. "I'd like to find out everything that's happened to you. Especially about the bear," he added: "You never told us the full story."

It was a long time since I had caught up with the Bethlehem Boys. Ages. Four new moons at least, and I was practically an adult – almost fourteen, with experience of life at its most rugged and challenging. They were eager to find out all they could. Consequently, I had a rapt audience; but my spirit had learnt caution, and a little humility. I was eager to boast in the Lord, and his goodness to me, but in my own exploits I was not quite so eager to boast. As a result, I did not cut as heroic a figure in my account as my admirers might have liked. It mattered not; they were content.

Each day of the festival, sacrifices and offerings were made to the Lord. Grain offerings, drink offerings, burnt offerings; gifts and free will offerings. Each family brought their gifts and presented them to the Lord. Priests from the tribe of Levi conducted and organised the ceremonies. They oversaw the sacrifices and divided the portions among the people. In my eyes, we were having a sacred meal with God.

His portion was consumed by smoke, our portion was consumed by ourselves. We, the people, brought the offerings, whether grain or meat, but God provided it, and, ultimately, it all belongs to Him.

The first and eighth day were days of complete rest. Even the stranger, even the alien and the slave could do no regular work. These two days were set apart to the Lord. In between these two days the festival continued, but normal patterns of life resumed: food-preparation; water-carrying; fuel-collection; etcetera. The basics of life still needed to be attended to.

So… the festival progressed. Singing was my favourite element. Also, I loved the stories taken from our history, well known as they were, and my spirit thrilled to the solemn prayers and rituals that accompanied the sacrifices: the blood on the altar, the lambs, the bullocks, the knives, the robes, the smoke from the sacrifice… the loaves of bread waved to the Lord.

These time-honoured, God emplaced rituals – they were part of our lives, and I embraced them. But… the singing…

When night came, the songs began in earnest. There were songs of triumph and songs of tragedy; songs of joy and sorrow; of praise and adoration; of meditation and contemplation; of exaltation and of entreaty. We were rich in our storehouses of song. Some songs were sung by skilled singers from the tribe of Levi, with the choruses carried by the whole assembly. Some were response songs, some were echo songs. The night rumbled with the rhythmic cadences. Our favourite songs were the ones we had learned in our mother's laps: 'Lilies'; 'The Doe of the Morning'; 'A Dove on Distant Oaks': these songs everyone knew. My all-time favourite was: 'Do Not Destroy' – because of its sweet, repetitive melody, and the heart-stirring chorus. When the assembly joined together to sing this song the stars seemed to come closer, the fire to burn brighter, and a sense of oneness and security joined our hearts.

"What greater privilege is there," Ishpah once asked me, "… than to bring praises to the Holy One? Surely it is the best thing in life that we can do."

In life… Life: that great mystery. Today we sing and praise and dwell securely; tomorrow we betray and steal, we envy and fight. War comes, famine approaches, our festivals are no longer observed, our belief fails. We worship idols, we fall sick, we become slaves and fugitives.

Where is our God then? Why has he abandoned us? Where is our hope? What hope is there?

But this year – my fourteenth – this year we dwell securely. We dance before the Lord like water lapping on the shores of Heaven. Our cisterns and barns are full; oil overflows every pot; grain spills; smoke ascends; even the young lions do not suffer want… this year.

*

Now – winter has passed. Now – I am back in the hills. And alone. And my flock has increased. I am by myself. There is no Sol, no Nimrod, no Badak. Just me and my shepherd's pipe and harp, sling and staff, pouch and water-skin. I am keeping my eyes open and keeping my distance from the other flocks and shepherds. Something is in the air.

One morning I stand on the brow of a cliff, gazing at the sun rising over the mountains of Moab. The latter rains have passed. Five months have passed since the Feast of Tabernacles. Sheep shearing time is nearly here. The crops: millet; peas; lentils; melons; cucumbers; grain – have all been planted – but not by me. The flax is ready to harvest. And – a lamb is missing from my flock. Where could it be, I wonder?

I become aware of a soft, growling noise beneath my very feet – almost a purring – and leap nimbly down onto the ledge below, knife and club at the ready. There, hidden beneath the overhang is a young lion. Well… what was I expecting? Climbing back up is not an option, and there is a lamb in its mouth, which drops to the ground as I land on the ledge. The lion places its foot on it, and snarls at me. There is no escape. Suddenly, I am Samson. My whole body – every fibre – is taut and tuned. Holding the beast with my eye, I lean forward and whisk the lamb away and fling it onto the crest above. Now, it is just me and it. Dispossessed and discomfited, the lion eyes me uncertainly. Then its ancient nature takes over and it springs at me! It seems to hang in the air – time has halted. Smoothly, I step to one side, grab the hair of its head, clasp it to my side and in the same motion draw Zeruiah's steel knife across its throat. When it hits the ground, it rises no more.

I become aware of a raking wound that runs down my side and my thigh. Blood is running freely. I raise my eyes to God – I know He is with me. But I am Samson no longer. Back to the lower pastures we go, my father's sheep and I.

I will bathe in the still waters. I will recover in the green pastures. And I will not share this account with Abishai, or Ishpah, or Sol, or even Zeruiah… I will keep this between

God and me – it is a seal of his guardianship – of his jealous care. I will indeed be watchful, but whom shall I fear? Only Him, who is my keeper.

Chapter 13
Ahinoam

I stayed in the lower pastures, not far from home, in an ancient olive grove, bleeding and weak, until late afternoon. Then, who should come along, twirling their slings, but – Insufferable and Inseparable – my two nephews: the future mighty men of our nation, Abishai and Joab. Their eyes lit up when they saw me, but it didn't take them long to realise something was amiss.

"What's the matter? What happened?" demanded Abishai. "You're hurt!"

"I slipped," I invented. "What are you doing here? Why aren't you harvesting the flax?"

"We are! We just got let off for a break. Show me what you did."

"It's nothing. By tomorrow I'll be over it. Tonight, I'll stay here to recover. Maybe you could bring me some food later. Don't tell anyone! I'm fine."

Joab said nothing. He looked unconvinced. They exchanged a look and then to my surprise they started to go away.

"We'll see what we can do," Abishai called: "Will you stay here?"

"I will," I assured them.

Sure enough, the terrible twosome completely ignored my request for secrecy, and before the chill of evening had arrived they returned, leading a troop of rescuers – my father, my mother, Zeruiah, Ishpah, not to mention a few other interested observers. A couple of my brothers and the old herb woman, Alesha, were among them. So much for secrecy! I lifted my eyes reproachfully to Heaven and readied myself to endure the concern and consolation that was approaching.

They carried me home.

"You will have to rest for several days, my son," my father instructed me. "You are weak and feverish. You have bled much. I thank the Lord that he sent Zeruiah's sons in your path. Your wounds have been washed in new wine and dressed with oil. Healing herbs have been bandaged to your wounds. Lie still."

"How long have I been asleep, father?"

"Since yesterday, when we found you."

"Who is caring for the sheep?"

"Not you, my son. Be still. Rest quietly. Here, drink this. We will bring you some food shortly."

He left the little room and low, eager voices could be heard in the other room. It was my nephews, eager to find out what had happened.

"Go home!" my father commanded them, speaking very quietly and firmly. "You may come back tomorrow at this time – but not before."

I smiled to myself as reluctant footsteps scuffed away. The poor boys! Twenty-four more hours to wait to find out. I felt my side and my hip gingerly. Mounds of healing herbs were lightly packed under a square of linen and held down by linen straps. It felt cool and clean. I needed to relieve myself. The chamber pot was handy – it was a long time since I had last used one.

Sleep came, and a dream. I was roaming in a beautiful garden, perfumed and tranquil, like the Garden of Eden. God was there – felt but not seen. The edges of the garden were suffused with a golden glow – and music – soul-stirring and inspiring – rose like thunderclouds over the mountains. I walked through the garden as if I belonged there, safe and secure amid lions and bears, and laid myself down on a mossy bank beside a stream. It was comfortable, and the water that trickled through my fingers sparkled with life. A tree stood tall above me, dappling the sunlight. Soft hands caressed my forehead gently… gently… and the music became low and sweet. Then, then – just when I was thirsting for more – the colours faded, the stream faded, the garden began to disappear – and I was returned to my couch of sheepskin and bracken, in the little ante-room of my father's house. I could feel a stray piece of straw sticking into my back, but, strangely, although the garden had gone, and the stream and the lions – the music and the stroking fingers were still with me. I opened my eyes. There before me, crouched next to me like an angel, was a girl of my own age. Something in her eyes said to me: "You are mine. You belong to me. I am looking after you." She looked at me confidently and lovingly. Such a look! And as our eyes held each other, she continued to sing the melody of my dream and to stroke my forehead.

"I am dreaming again," I told her: "I hope I don't wake up."

She laughed. "You are a sick little boy who has been fighting lions, and now I am in charge of you. Do you know who I am?"

"No." I shook my head.

"I am Ahinoam of Jezreel, daughter of Phineas, son of Eliud. My sister and I escaped when the Philistines raided our village. We arrived the other day and are now servants in your father's house. I am your slave."

"Is this real?" I asked, curiously.

"It is. Does this feel real?" she pressed gently on my bandages and laughed when I winced with pain. Tears came to my eyes. She saw them and her expression softened. "Shall I prepare you some food?"

"Yes, please do. But first, where is my father and mother, and how do you know I have been fighting with lions?"

"They are with the harvest. It is my duty to prepare the food, and I have seen the lion's skin."

"I don't understand."

"They found it this morning – your cousins… or nephews – whatever they are. They went looking for the lion that attacked you. Obviously, the claw marks on your body are those of a lion, and they found it, and killed it, and…"

"They what?"

"They found it and killed it – with the help of Sol the hunter – and the skin is pegged out on Sol's roof. Everyone has been to see it – even me!"

I was lost for words: confused, bemused, exhausted, but strangely comforted. My secret was safe. I glanced towards the chamber pot. It was empty and clean. Ahinoam followed my glance and smiled.

"I am you slave," she repeated, softly; "But I am also in charge of you. I have to look after you and make you well. Now, relax and be still, as your father instructed. I will be close by if you need me."

A parting stroke of the head, a caressing look, and she left the room. I wriggled deeper into my bed and felt that annoying piece of straw disturb my peace.

"Ahinoam!" I called: "There's a bit of straw in my bed. Could you move it?"

"Yes, master," she smiled, gracefully re-entering the room.

I saw that she was slender and timid, like a fawn in the forest, and she carried the mantle of sorrow and the scars of flight. She had found a safe haven in our home – but how safe, and for how long?

"Where is it?" she enquired.

I pointed. I lifted myself up on my elbows with an effort, and she ran her hand between my back and the lambskin in search of the straw. It was an intimate moment that caught us both unawares. A thrill passed through my whole body. A thrill of longing and of yearning, as sweet and rapturous as anything I have ever felt. She felt it too, I am sure.

"Here it is," she announced, producing the straw: "Now lie back, you sick little boy. Is that better? Lie still now. Relax. Have some more sleep. It won't be long before the family returns, I have much to do."

I watched her leave, graceful and resolute, and my heart was stirred with a mixture of emotions: desire, longing, admiration; pity; love… even love.

"One day, father, I would like to marry Ahinoam."

Many days had passed. I was better.

All the village knew how Sol had killed the lion. Abishai and Joab knew better, as did Sol. With native cunning they had hatched this story in order to keep Jesse's son out of the spotlight. Jesse's son – the rumoured king-to-be – was already held in suspicion by the shepherds of Benjamin and this suspicion needed to be allayed. Lion-killing would only add fuel to the flames of their fear. Whose idea was it, one might wonder, this story of finding and killing my lion? Abishai's? Surely not. He was too plain for such a scheme. Joab? Well, possibly: he was only ten years old, but a proven strategist. Sol? More than likely. He knew at first hand the enmity borne towards me by Benjamin, and he was a grown man, a hunter and a father – and well versed in the ways of the world and the art of survival.

"Father?"

"Yes, my son David."

"One day, I would like to marry Ahinoam."

"I know. I am old but I am not blind. One day, this may be so, but I have unexpected news for you. While you were sick, we received this message from the court of King Saul. You are wanted. Someone has spoken for you. King Saul wants you to attend on him. You will wait on the king. You are to leave tomorrow. Behold – this is the king's seal. Ethan will travel with you. I have prepared provisions. May the God of Abraham and Isaac and Jacob watch over you."

The next day we left, taking a donkey which was loaded with bread, a skin of wine, and a young goat. Also – my harp and pipe, my sling and club and knife, and the other basic necessities of life. Ahinoam watched me go with sadness and with pride. The family farewelled me. Ethan and I left at dawn. We were travelling to Gibeah, the city of Saul, in Benjamin. Sol accompanied us. He knew the way.

Chapter 14
To the Court of King Saul

We reached Gibeah via the mountain tracks around midday. On the way we kept a sharp eye out for Cush and Doeg, King Saul's chief shepherds. We had last seen them on our journey to Moab, and well knew the violent hostility they nurtured towards me. But the God of Abraham, Isaac and Jacob gave us safe passage, as my father had trusted he would. Our way north led us close to the ancient fortress city once known as Jerusalem – and now known as Jebus. The Jebusites were hardy and warlike. Their city was still unconquered and existed in the midst of our Promised Land like an island. The city of Jebus sat on the boundary between Judah and Benjamin, and neither of our tribes had the will to attempt a conquest. It was too hard – we had enough challenges.

"Let us leave the road," Sol advised, "… and go around the mountains until we have passed the city. We don't want to fall into the hands of the Jebusites."

"Why is this so?" I demanded, as much to myself as to Sol and Ethan. "This is our land; we are one nation. Why is Judah fearful of Benjamin? Why is brother against brother? Why are strangers in our midst? Why are Philistines keeping us in constant fear? Why do we have to turn off the track in our own land?"

Sol looked at me with compassion and understanding.

"Suffer it to be so for now," he said quietly: "It may please God to bring about change, but for now we must act wisely. What are a few more mountains?"

I laughed, but I cast my youthful eyes over the city of Jebus in the distance and felt it was wrong. It was an offence to the God of Israel. These impostors should not live in our midst. It should not be!

Be this as it may, we travelled a few more mountains, then re-joined our original track and carried on northwards for a little longer.

"That's Gibeah there, on that hilltop," Sol pointed, as we rounded a bend.

We gazed at it with interest. The city of Saul: Gibeah. Fifty years ago, it had been torn to the ground and burnt and plundered. Every was soul destroyed. And by whom? The Philistines? The Amalekites? Ammon? Moab? Edom?

No, none of these – it was Judah, Ephraim, Gad, Dan… in other words – us. Their own brothers.

How could such an outrage be possible? How could brother turn against brother? No wonder God nearly lost patience with us in the desert and was ready to destroy us all. The grumbling and unbelief of our people was legendary. It was Moses who had stood in the gap on that occasion. He pleaded – and God relented. We were indeed a stiff-necked people. No wonder tension still existed between Benjamin and Judah.

Truly, I had felt safer in Moab than I did right here in my own land. But fortunately, there was now a greater evil that caused us to draw together as a nation, and to put old resentments to one side. This greater evil was – the Philistines. Our nation was hard pressed by them. Like a tide their oppression ebbed and flowed. They raided, they set up garrisons, they launched full-scale battles, they demanded tribute, they took our weapons – they were a powerful people. They lived by the sea. They had chariots and horses, iron swords and spears. It might seem surprising that in all these generations of fighting, they had not wiped us all out. They certainly kept us underfoot. Maybe that's what they preferred.

The city of Gibeah had been rebuilt. Saul had been chosen as king twenty-six years ago. His reign was devoted to defending Israel from the attacks of our enemies. After a shaky start he now inspired a sense of unity that caused men from every tribe to flock to his standard whenever danger threatened.

It had not always been so. In the twentieth year of his reign, Philistines came in great numbers to King Saul's very door, in the valley of Michmash, and camped all around. The army of Israel was terrified and quickly decreased in number, as men deserted and fled into the nearby hills to hide. Only six hundred valiant men remained and destruction loomed. It was at this point that a saviour appeared, who turned the course of our nation's destiny and strengthened the hearts of Israel. After this great deliverance, the tribes of Israel flocked willingly to the royal standard.

So – who was this saviour? Samuel, the prophet? Abner, the commander-in-chief? Cush, the terrible? No. It was Saul's own son – Jonathan. He was aged eighteen, only ten years my senior.

In our darkest hour he responded to the prompting of God. He climbed a cliff with his armour-bearer. The Philistines above looked down and mocked the two climbers… and let them get to the top. Then – miraculously – our heroes overcame them and a mindless panic set in. The Philistines fled. They fought among themselves, discarded their weapons, and were slaughtered all the way back to the coast by our triumphant army. It was a panic sent by God, and Jonathan's words to his armour-bearer were immortalised in the folklore of our firesides:

"Come, you and I, let us climb this cliff and attack these uncircumcised heathens. Nothing can hinder the Lord from saving, whether by many, or by few!"

"Do all that you will, I am with you heart and soul," came the armour bearer's famous response.

They climbed the unclimbable cliff and the Lord gave the enemy into their hands. It was the talk of Israel. Now, every boy wanted to climb that cliff. Jonathan was a national hero and his father's reign was strengthened and vindicated. And, here I was today, at the gates of Gibeah, with the seal of Saul in my hand, about to enter into the service of the king… or… dread thought: about to be executed on suspicion of being a rival to the throne.

I explained my business to the gatekeeper and was taken to see the King – leaving Sol and Ethan holding the donkey.

Entering this grim city was strange and disconcerting. It felt laden with menace, as if the very walls were looking at me with disfavour. But – there was nothing for it but to follow my chaperone and hold on to the Lord. My breath came more quickly as we progressed. We wended our way through the maze of houses until we reached the walled palace – the citadel – which was built into the highest and most impregnable part of the city's outer wall, complete with look-outs and a tower overhead. On the other side of the palace gate was a large courtyard with rooms beyond. We stated our business to King Saul's personal attendant and I was conducted up to a room in the tower.

Shafts of dusty light came in through narrow windows on three sides and met in the centre of this room. Between the windows it was dim and shadowy. I did not see the king until my eyes adjusted. He was lying on a low bed, gazing at me with great weariness. His face was gaunt and haunted. The attendant shuffled uneasily. Slowly, the king rose to his feet, towering over me. I prostrated myself before him, then rose submissively and awaited his pleasure.

I looked into his eyes and met his gaze. As I did so, a feeling of intense love and compassion and privilege swept over me. This was the man, the anointed of God, the lamp of Israel, whom I was called to serve. The dark eyes read the homage in my eyes. He saw my eager desire to serve and the sweet loyalty and pride that I felt for him, and the weariness in his face disappeared. Suddenly he looked young and strong and commanding. What medicine it is to find love and loyalty in the breast of another! The gaze of the king rested on me comfortably, and I lowered my eyes to permit him all the time he wished. After a little while he placed his hands on my shoulders and I lifted my head.

"Whose son are you, young man?" he asked.

"I am the son of your servant, Jesse of Bethlehem," I replied.

Chapter 15
Within the Walls

My life changed from that moment.

I loved the king as a father, and he loved me as a son. But – he was a man under intense spiritual oppression – and never more so than at this time in his reign, when war was *not* threatening.

Our enemies had been pushed back to their borders and an uneasy peace was in the land. Saul had entrusted the oversight of the nation to his son Jonathan, the heir apparent, and to Abner, his long-standing general. Abner was Saul's cousin. He was twenty years younger than Saul and an adept and capable general. Customarily, Saul would lead the army with Abner at his side, and great victories had been won in the last six years since the battle of Michmash. But now – there was no immediate threat – and Saul stayed home while his son and his general kept an eye on things.

Staying home was bad for King Saul. He had too much leisure. An evil spirit from God tormented him.

How could this be, you ask?

In our culture, and rightly so, all things were considered to come from God: defeat; victory; joy; sorrow; famine; plenty. It was all spelt out in his law – 'If you fully obey me, you will be blessed, but if you do not obey you will be cursed'. Saul had not obeyed; everyone knew this. The prophet Samuel had given him clear directions from God regarding a certain matter, and he had failed to fulfil them, knowingly. And it was not the first time he had failed to obey the divine command. From this point, God took his Holy Spirit away from him, and Saul became subject to self-doubt and paranoid fears and suspicions. An evil spirit, sent from God, tormented him.

This was the reason I had been sent for. One of Saul's young and compassionate attendants (can you guess who?) had suggested that perhaps his soul could be soothed at these times of torment by music played by a sensitive and inspired hand. The young attendant had suggested me, the son of Jesse, as the perfect choice: "He knows how to play the harp. He is a brave man and a warrior. He speaks well and is a fine-looking man, and the Lord is with him."

What a recommendation! A brave man and a warrior. Me! At fourteen years old. Perhaps Michael was looking to the future with the eyes of faith. But anyhow, here I was, and – I was right for the job. I could feel the onset of these attacks on my master, and the soothing balm of my presence, and of God's spirit, would become infused with the music of my harp, and bring him solace and reprieve. Consequently, I became a favourite. King Saul sent word to my father:

'Allow David to remain in my service, for I am pleased with him.'

My father consented. Well… what else could he do? And the king made me one of his armour bearers. I was among the retinue of attendants and bodyguards who accompanied him wherever he went. He always took his spear, helmet and shield, on even the smallest expedition, and I became familiar with the towns and battlegrounds that we visited. The spiritual attacks became less and less.

*

One year passed. Then another. Sheep-shearing time was at hand and I approached the king with a request of my own.

"Rise my son," he said, kindly: "What is it that you request?"

"If it seems good to you my lord, my father is old and in need of my services and sheep-shearing time will soon be here. May I return for a season to help my family?"

King Saul looked at me gravely from his simple wooden throne of state. The raven locks streaked with grey framed his large and angular face: the prominent nose and chin, the thick lips, the deep sunk eyes. "David," he half whispered, "you are like an angel of God to me. How can I manage without you? Yet, I will permit you to go, but for a season only. Return and celebrate with me at the Passover Festival. I will need you then."

"Thank you, my lord. The King is like an angel of heaven. I will indeed return, as you have commanded."

I bowed, left his presence with due ceremony, and prepared myself for my journey home. Home! How I looked forward to re-joining my loved ones. What stories I could tell them now!

Chapter 16
An Impetuous Youth

"Tell us everything!" my father commanded.

An eager gathering had assembled in the courtyard to learn all they could about Bethlehem's favourite son. Zeruiah and her boys were there, naturally; also, my sister Abigail and her son Amasa, and several of my brothers – but not Eliab, even though he was in town… no doubt he had better things to do than listen to anything I might say. Ishpah was there; also Sol, Ethan, Ahinoam – my sweet little escapee – and there were lots of others… sitting on the walls, standing in the doorways, banked up in the corners. The Bethlehem Boys were there; it was a welcome fit for a king, and a perfect spring evening into the bargain – still and starry.

It was cold in the hills, but it was warm in the crowded courtyard. Wine and bread were offered around and the scene was illuminated by torches of old linen and pitch, by guttering oil lamps and by the host of Heaven.

"Tell us everything! First, how is King Saul to you? Does he treat you well? And where do you live? And what is the palace like?"

"The palace is cold and dark. It is much smaller than the king of Moab's. I live nearby with Michael and other attendants. King Saul lives in the palace with his family."

"He has many cares. Is he a happy man?"

"No. He is not. He is greatly wearied by burdens of spirit and of state, but he is a good man, or he tries to be. He is good to me. He is like a second father."

"Have you been to war yet?" a boyish voice piped up eagerly.

My father cast a severe glance at the impetuous one and continued to speak: "I am glad, my son, that the king treats you well."

"He does indeed, Father. I believe it is God's will for me to be there."

Ishpah nodded sagely.

"I am able to comfort the king when he is burdened in spirit." I added.

"How do you do this? What actually happens?"

"Well, at times he is heavily oppressed by a tormenting spirit, and his life becomes a burden, and his face becomes gaunt and fearful. When this happens… I play my harp for him."

"How long do these times of torment last?"

"In the past – several days. Once he used to shut himself into the tower and his servants would fear to approach him. But these days it's not so bad. That's why I am able to come and visit you."

"So you play your harp – and this helps him?"

"It does. It is the Lord that helps him – through the music."

"Have you been to any battles?" the boyish voice squeaked.

"It is a position of great privilege that the Lord has given you, my son," my father pronounced, casting another disapproving look at the interrupter.

Ishpah nodded sagely.

"Have you met Jonathan?" the boyish voice squeaked, insistently.

"Have you met Jonathan?" my father echoed unexpectedly, picking up on the youngster's enthusiasm.

"Not really. He is not often there. I have mostly been with Saul while Jonathan and Abner are away with the army. I met him once, briefly, and he treated me with great warmth, since he knows I am of service to his father."

"And whereabouts are the armies now?"

"Have you met Abner?"

"Shhh! Joab! That's enough of your noise. Be quiet."

"Abner is stationed up north, in Ephraim, to keep an eye on the Philistines, and Jonathan is over to the east of the Jordan, watching out for the Ammonites."

"That means we are unprotected from the south," one of the elders observed: "How typical! We in Judah are left to look after ourselves. We have the Edomites, the Moabites, the Amalekites and the Philistines on our doorstep… and King Saul of Benjamin gives us no heed, except to take our best fighting men for himself, and leave us weakened and exposed!"

"God is our protection," Ishpah remonstrated: "God – and these wild hills he has given us. King Saul is doing all he can, and if we support him, he will support us. He is a valiant man."

The elder grunted, and a muffled rumble of discontent rippled through the older members of the gathering. They all felt that our tribe Judah was getting a bad deal. It was payback for the past, they thought. I disagreed. I knew that King Saul was doing all he could.

"He *is* a valiant man," I muttered, defensively.

There was a moment's uneasiness in our gathering. Any second now and the whole scene would disintegrate into violent disagreement and bickering – even violence! We were Hebrews, after all. Then, like a shaft of peculiar light…

"How tall is King Saul?" came that petulant, boyish voice.

This odd and disconnected question somehow diffused the tension, and a guffaw of manly laughter, accompanied by the higher pitched merriment of the women and children, swept the moment of disagreement away. The good mood returned – but the voice was not to be denied.

"How tall is King Saul?" came the question again, louder and more insistent.

"Alright, Joab!" I responded, yielding at last to his importunity. "I will tell you how tall King Saul is. He towers over me like a bear. He towers over everybody! He is a head taller than the tallest man in Israel."

Joab whistled. "And how tall is Jonathan?" he demanded.

"That's enough!" my brother Abinadab snapped irritably. "Keep quiet or go to bed!"

Zeruiah glared at Abinadab: "I'll manage my own sons, if it pleases you!" she flashed.

"Jonathan is quite tall," I interposed, for the sake of peace: "As tall as Eliab, my brother, at least."

"And a goodly man indeed!" my father declared. "And you, my son, how you have grown in these last two years! Why, when first I set my eyes on you – I could hardly believe it was you! Are you not as tall as Eliab yourself?"

"Hardly, my father," I answered bashfully. "But I am getting there."

"You *are* indeed – my son David. Oh – how good it is that you can be with us for a season! Your brothers are going back to the army in the next few days, and I will need your help."

"It is my pleasure, my father. I am grateful to be home with you."

"We are grateful to have you," my father assured me.

Ishpah nodded, sagely.

*

I was home for three weeks. Three short weeks. I oversaw the work in the fields and kept an eye on the flocks. I was the only unmarried son in the family now, since my other brothers, now soldiers, had all been married in the last few years. As a result, I was now my father's right hand.

The day before my return to King Saul a sense of dissatisfaction crept over me like a morning mist – it had been building for months.

"Father, when am I going to be married?" I asked, gazing wistfully at Ahinoam as she set off to the well after our household devotions. She had become more beautiful in the last year – and was a picture of grace in the early morning sun, with the tall water pot on her shoulder. She loved me. My heart pounded with sudden longing: "When, father?" I pleaded.

"Not for another year or two. You are not like your brothers, David. Your life is not your own. You are bound up with the purposes of God and you are a servant in the court of the king. You must be patient." His expression softened as he saw my disappointment and he smiled: "Keep trusting in God, my son. All will be well. Why don't you take time off today and seek out your old friend Ishpah? He may be able to help you to see more clearly."

*

I found Ishpah weeding his cucumbers. "Shalom, my son," he greeted me.

"Shalom, my father," I responded: "tell me, Ishpah. Why can I not be married?"

He straightened up and looked at me with those eyes I remembered so well – still dark and shining as if lit up from within. "Of course you cannot be married! God has a plan for you, and at this point, you need to be listening to him, not building your own nest. Is not your life full enough already? You are King Saul's trusted servant and companion, and you have duties and responsibilities to fulfil. To everything there is a season. Recognise, David, that for you this is a season of waiting on the Lord, not marrying."

I was dumbfounded. For once I had nothing to say. Ishpah gave me a piercing glance that cut through the layers of self-pity and dissatisfaction that had begun to enfold me.

"Is Michael married?" he demanded. "Is he not content and privileged to serve the King? And in only a small capacity, and with no release! You need to learn from Michael!

"Have you become important in your own eyes? This is a serious error. Your clear path is to honour God – in word, in deed and in heart. 'Those who honour me, I will honour', says our Lord, the living God. And how will you honour him? By doing with all your heart all that he calls you to do. With all your heart! Repent of your dissatisfaction and serve Him eagerly, as you have always done in the past. Why do you think he chose you? Why do you think he called his prophet Samuel to anoint you with holy oil?

"Because – you were small in your own eyes but you magnified the Lord. Because – you saw with the eyes of the spirit and not the eyes of the flesh; and because – you were not like other men – petty, dissatisfied and earthy. He chose you because you have a heart after Him.

"You have a heart after God, David. Keep it. Cherish it. Watch over it. For out of the heart flow the wellsprings of life. Let your springs be true, let them be pure, giving glory to the one who chose you, and who will keep you, and provide for you, and, in due course, will give you all things. Only remember, God honours those who honour him. Trust, be patient, rejoice in the path he has marked out for you. Walk it joyfully and humbly. Now go… in peace."

With this inspiring exhortation still ringing in my ears, and eating a cucumber given to me by my ancient mentor, I returned to Gibeah in a new frame of spirit. Yes, Ishpah was right. I had fallen into the trap of expecting more – and had forgotten how blessed I already was. I was ashamed of myself.

My life in the court of Saul had not been easy, it is true. There had been sneers, veiled glances, malicious whispers. In fact, the clean air of the mountains was much better than the heavy oppression of the court. Also, there was King Saul with his unpredictability and his spiritual need. Maybe it was not to be wondered at that I had been laid so low. All that harp playing, all that worship drawn from my precious store – and little opportunity to seek the Lord and be still in his presence.

When does true worship stop being true and start being empty? I had come close to that point. My visit to Bethlehem had come in the nick of time. Saul, my master, had found spiritual firmness just as my own spirit had begun to crumble – and if it was not for Ishpah, I may never have realised this. But – behind Ishpah was Yahweh, and it was he – Yahweh – who had released me and restored me. Now, as I returned to Gibeah to the intrigues and uncertainties of the king's court, it was with new confidence. I was armed with new weapons – the weapons of humility and sweetness of spirit.

Truly, I would need them.

Chapter 17
Deep Calling to Deep

It was my fourth journey between Bethlehem and Gibeah so I had no need of a guide. Nonetheless my father provided three companions for my safety. A strange thing happened as we took the long mountain detour around the city of the Jebusites. On previous occasions my spirit had been outraged at these hard-headed aliens living in our midst, like snakes in the garden – but, this time, it was different. This time – I felt that I could see beyond the present; in my spirit I could see beyond the years, as if looking over distant mountains – and I could see that Jebus was really only a mirage, shimmering in the sands of time. One day, in a moment, in a twinkling of an eye – it would be Jebus no longer. No longer Jebus, the flint-hard rock of reproach – but Jerusalem – the City of God. The sands would shift, the mirage would shimmer, and Jebus would be no more. I gasped, as a sense of prophetic insight threatened to sweep me off the mountain top and bear me into the beyond. Power too mighty to be contained tugged at the fibres of my being. I felt the great weight of God's purposes bearing down upon me – too mighty for me – too big, and – and yet… not mine to bring about – and not mine to agonise over. My part was simple – just to guard my heart… and to serve…

The little hill-top city of Gibeah came into view and before long we were at the gates. My companions took my few possessions to my quarters and returned home to Bethlehem. As I walked through the well-known streets that familiar sense of oppression began to creep over me. Anxious faces greeted me from within the citadel. The King… the King! I was needed urgently.

Taking a firm hold on my faith in God and on my harp, I followed the courtier through the palace check-points back to the familiar room. There lay the king, his face etched with exhaustion and fear, his spear upright in its holder next to the bed. He sat up wildly as we entered, and the courtier backed away nervously. I approached the king gently and my presence brought peace and comfort to his troubled spirit. He visibly relaxed. I prostrated myself in homage, kissed the ring on his hand, and began to play. The courtier flashed me a wondering look – a mixture of confusion, relief, disbelief – even jealousy – and left… to spread the news of the king's impending recovery among his fellows. With the courtier gone the atmosphere became peaceful and serene; bird-calls fluttered through the sunlit lattices; bees hummed soothingly in the flowering vines that crept up the high stone walls; sweet perfumes of early summer wafted into the cheerless room and chased away the stark figments of madness that had been strutting there so recently, and in such force. King Saul lay recumbent, regathering his strength and his spirit. The gauntness disappeared. At length he opened his eyes and looked directly at me:

"Whose son are you, young man?"

The question startled me.

"I am the son of your servant, Jesse of Bethlehem," I replied.

The king nodded. A shadow crossed his face.

"Play on," he ordered huskily: "I will be well."

Chapter 18
Puzzles from the Past

"Hear O Israel: The Lord is One.

And you shall love the Lord your God – With all your heart and with all your soul and with all your mind…"

It was Passover. I was listening to the sonorous voice of Ahimelech, the high priest.

"Remember – I am the Lord your God. Who brought you out of the land of Egypt. Out of the house of bondage. You shall have no other gods before me…

Remember…"

The Day of Passover was a memorial service over two hundred years old, commemorating the Lord's release of Israel from Egypt. For each small group of worshipers, a lamb without blemish was to be sacrificed. Sandals on our feet and staff in hand, as if ready for a journey – this is how we were to prepare ourselves. The meat was first roasted and then eaten in haste with bitter herbs. For seven days, only unleavened bread was to be eaten. No leaven was to be even touched. Why? you might wonder – and what is 'leaven' anyway? Well – leaven is dough with yeast in it – and our practice was to always keep a lump of leavened dough aside from today's batch for tomorrow's – so that tomorrow's dough would rise.

"A little leaven leavens the whole lump," Ishpah explained to me.

But why no leaven at Passover? This was the question I wanted an answer to. I already knew Ishpah's explanation, but I wanted to find out from an actual priest. The previous fifteen days at Saul's city had been spent consecrating ourselves in preparation for Passover, and in that time I was able to approach Ahimelech the high priest.

Ahimelech was from the tribe of Levi as were all our priests. He lived in the priest's town of Nob, close to Gibeah. I had once visited the priest's town of Nob with King Saul and his entourage – and seen the tabernacle of the Lord: the tent of Yahweh. It was a great honour to accompany the king and to enter the outer court of the tabernacle. I beheld the ancient artefacts: the great horned brazen altar, the huge copper water bowl, the brass tongs and scoops and pans and knives.

The great altar was a sacred and holy edifice. It was a place of sacrifice and it was also a place of refuge. A man could flee into the outer court and lay hold on the horns of the altar and be safe from his enemies. We had played a game as children based on this. How secure it had felt to grab the rock of refuge and call out "Kadesh!" In our language this word meant: 'holy' – in other words – safe, secure, protected…

I stood that day within the curtained-off outer court – and it reminded me of my people's forty-year sojourn in the desert. That was the time when the Lord gave Moses His design for the Tabernacle. How strange and alien that sojourn in the desert must have been! Beyond the outer court where I now stood was the inner sanctuary – the Holy Place. I looked longingly at the curtains that screened off this sanctuary. I would love to have seen behind those curtains – but the golden artefacts they concealed were not for my eyes: the altar of incense, the golden table of offering, and the seven-branched lamp-stand, always alight – these were not to be gazed on. This was the Holy Place. Beyond the Holy Place was – the Holy of Holies. Only the high priest could enter this special room, and only once a year.

The Holy of Holies contained the Ark of the Covenant – it was the most precious visible token of Yahweh's covenant with his people. The Ark was a wooden chest, skilfully made and overlaid with gold. Out of either end of the golden lid two golden angels rose and hovered. The space between the two angels was known as the mercy seat.

"Our God is a God of mercy and justice," Ishpah never tired of telling me: "He is greatly to be honoured."

In size the Ark was no bigger than a travelling chest. It contained the stone tablets of our law, and it also contained Aaron's staff which had budded in the wilderness, as well as a sample of the manna which had fallen in the desert, perfectly preserved. But alas – the Ark was not there! The Tabernacle lacked its crowning glory. Each day the priests replenished the lampstand with oil, washed and consecrated themselves and made burnt offerings; and each week they replaced the bread of God's presence… however, within the Holy of Holies – that special place where only the high priest could go – the most special thing of all: the Ark of the Covenant… was missing.

Ishpah, who knew everything and more about matters like this, explained to me why this was so. Long, long ago, when

Samuel was a boy – Israel had lost a battle to the Philistines, and the Ark of the Covenant (which had accompanied our army) was captured. Great was the distress of our nation. How could this be? After some months, however, the Philistines returned the Ark – because wherever it went in their land, disease broke out – and their gods of stone fell over and broke in pieces. Our people rejoiced to see the Ark returning but foolishly forgot to treat it with reverence. They opened the chest and looked inside. This was sacrilege. Yahweh destroyed them. After this no one knew what to do. Eventually a devoted man was consecrated to watch over the Ark in a hill village in Judah. It was still there.

So why, you might wonder, was the Ark – the jewel of the tabernacle – never returned to its rightful place? Fear, Ishpah said. Fear of further outbreaks of Yahweh's wrath and fear of the instability of the times. For example, the previous shrine of Shiloh had been destroyed by invaders, but thankfully the tabernacle and its contents had been moved to the village of Nob beforehand… but how secure was anywhere when we were hemmed in by our enemies on all sides? So: the priests of our nation continued to serve the Lord; they performed the rituals and officiated at the feasts – while the Ark of God's presence remained in obscurity somewhere in the hills of Judah.

It was a puzzle. Lots of things were a puzzle. But – we were a puzzling people. Our lives were full of riddles and contradictions. The most puzzling question of all was why had God chosen *us*, of all people, to be his chosen nation? I asked Ishpah this question and his answer was very peculiar.

"Perhaps Yahweh chose us to show that if there can be hope for us – there can be hope for everyone," he responded.

Now that I found puzzling indeed. Which reminds me. Leaven. Why no leaven at the Passover Feast?

I asked Ahimelech, the high priest: "Leaven," he answered, "is a symbol that God uses for hardness of heart; for clinging to old attitudes; for the puffed-up wisdom of man; and for pride. The Feast of Passover and the Feast of Unleavened Bread is about beginning a new day with God – putting aside the old; clinging to Him; venturing into new pastures with Him – untainted by the old. It is about setting oneself aside for God's plans and purposes."

I was impressed. His answer was much like Ishpah's. However, I was still puzzled:

"Does this actually happen?" I asked. "Will we begin again as new, without the taints of the past?"

"No, my son," came the response: "…but we will try. And God will understand. But true renewal will not begin until Shiloh himself comes."

"Who is Shiloh?" I whispered.

"The One who is to come."

At this point I went into a dream. There were two Shilohs, this I knew: one was the ancient resting-place of the tabernacle where Samuel had grown up – now destroyed; and the other Shiloh was the Man of God that Yahweh would one day send – the seed of the woman. The promised one. The Saviour.

I wondered… if perhaps… I might be him. Shiloh. The promised one. I could imagine myself leading the people, just as I had led my father's sheep – leading them with power and might, with wisdom and compassion… and speaking to them in words of inspiration, uniting their hearts and infusing them with the spirit of worship unto our God. I would teach them to sing psalms again – especially my own – and to take Yahweh at his word. Did he not say that those who honour him He would honour? It was so easy – so obvious. Why this ceaseless striving with our enemies and each other when a highway of holiness would lead us all to the Lord in peace and security? The warmth of my dream cooled as I became aware of a malevolent gaze directed at me from the shadows. It was Doeg the Edomite, King Saul's chief shepherd. He was delivering the lambs for the Passover ceremony. A more cruel and rapacious face I had never seen.

Hovering next to Doeg was Cush the Benjamite. He knew me; he hated me; he suspected me. Even now they might be devising some foul plot. They had it in for me, I could tell. I left – and joined Michael on the roof at our place of abode. He was fifteen now – one year younger than me – and his sweet spirit was like balm to my soul.

"Be careful," he counselled: "King Saul loves you, so you are safe – but the king is easily swayed. Take nothing for granted. Seek the Lord at all times. Seek the good of the king. Be diligent and whole-hearted at all times. When are you going to write another psalm?"

"Right now," I responded: "There is time. What better occupation for me?"

"I will write it; you create it," my little friend responded.

"Do you think that creating a psalm is as easy as pouring out water?" I demanded, affectionately.

"For you, yes. Especially now, at this moment. I can see by the light in your eyes that this is the very time for it."

"You are right," I agreed, soberly. "My heart is full: of hope and inspiration, of longing and of dread – and of joyful confidence in the Lord. Quickly – get your pen and ink and parchment. I am ready."

Michael readied himself and transcribed my psalm. It poured out like water:

"Unto thee do I cry O Lord my rock…
Do not be silent unto me.
For if you are silent to me
I will become like those who go down to the pit.
Hear the voice of my supplication
As I cry to you for help,
As I lift my hands towards your holy sanctuary.
Take me not away with the wicked
And with those who practice evil…
Who speak peace with their neighbours
While iniquity lurks in their hearts.
Repay them according to their works;
Give them according to their evil designs;
Render to them what they deserve.
Because they have no regard for the works of the Lord
And the operation of his hands –
He shall demolish them and never rebuild them.
Blessed be the Lord
For he has heard my heartfelt cry!
The Lord is my strength and my shield –
My heart trusts in him and I am helped:
Therefore, my heart leaps for joy,
And with my song I will praise him…"

"Is that it?" Michael enquired, sweating over his parchment.

"Not quite—"

"The Lord is the strength of his people,

A fortress of salvation for his anointed ones.

O save your people and bless your inheritance;

Be our shepherd and carry us in your arms forever."

"Now it is finished!"

"It *is* like a stream," Michael declared, as he added a final flourish: "I am going to copy it out neatly and add it to our collection."

"Can you really spare more parchment?"

"I serve the king's secretary – what better use for parchment than this?"

I smiled. We waited in silence on the Lord, as the shadows lengthened. How sweet was our companionship. Later that afternoon I returned to the royal court, keeping a watchful eye out for the hirelings of Saul – Doeg and Cush. These two shepherds had returned to the hills I was relieved to learn. When I attended on Saul, he was sober in spirit but not mad. He talked to me that night, as if I was a close adviser and confidant. His flashing eye and great physical presence made me understand how he had managed to forge a united nation from the loose conglomeration of the twelve argumentative tribes that he had been chosen to govern. Truly, he was the Lord's anointed. Somehow – he had drawn our fractious people to himself and, over time, gained ascendance over our enemies, to the point where all of Israel looked to his leadership, and rallied to his banner.

The day of Passover came. Ahimelech conducted the ceremony. The king's party consisted of Jonathan and Abner and their families. I was with a group of young servants and attendants. Abiathar, the son of the high priest, led our group. He was my own age. Like his father Ahimelech, Abiathar was filled with faith. Born into privilege and responsibility he had embraced our teachings whole-heartedly. It warmed my heart to see the fire of faith burning in another's breast and my high-flown hopes and aspirations of the previous afternoon were rekindled. We became friends, Abiathar and I. We had much in common.

The seven days of the Feast of Unleavened Bread which followed Passover were cut short. The Philistines, timing their stroke with cunning, knowing we were otherwise engaged, began to mass their armies around the neighbourhood of Gath, to the south-west.

Immediately the call to Israel went out; beacons were lit; and the Hebrews rallied to Saul at Gibeah.

"I will come with you, my father," I entreated the king. "I will be your right hand."

"You will not, my son David," the king denied me. "I cannot risk you in battle so soon. Return to your father in Bethlehem. Be *his* right hand. He has other sons who will rally to the call – older, stronger… and less precious to me. Go immediately, this very day. You have rendered me valuable service. God go with you. I will be well."

Chapter 19
An Unexpected Mission

I returned to Bethlehem feeling frustrated. More than half of our men had left the area to join the army and here was I – sixteen years old, fit, strong, eager for battle and of military age – consigned by the king to come home and look after the sheep. As if I was only a boy. It was humbling. David – armour-bearer to the king – sent home. It was frustrating! Had I not trained under Abner? Had I not competed against the best slingers of Gibeah – who could sling both right and left-handed at a hair and not miss – and won? All the world was in action – beacons blazing, swords flashing, feet tramping – and I was to have no part in it, except to stay at home with the old and the infirm, the women and the children, and wonder how the battle was going.

For two weeks, I wondered how the battle was going and still no news. Only rumours. At the end of this time, I was required to witness a rite of circumcision being performed on one of my nephews. He was eight days old. Jonadab was his name, the son of Shammah my brother, who was with King Saul.

Our law required that all males should be circumcised on the eighth day after birth. God had given Abraham this command. The cutting away of the foreskin of the penis was an outward sign of our nation's being set apart to Yahweh. Every man of Israel and every foreign slave – was to be circumcised. I witnessed the ceremony on behalf of my absent brother. The operation required a high degree of skill and care and I watched with interest and empathy. Hands were washed with olive oil soap and rinsed in freshly drawn water. A flint knife, freshly splintered, was used to cut away the fold of skin. Blood flowed, the baby cried. Within hours the infant was comforted and in only a few days healing was complete.

When our nation first entered Canaan, under the leadership of Joshua, there was a mass circumcision: the males born in the forty-year trek through the wilderness were all uncircumcised – why, I don't know. But I'm glad I wasn't among them. On that day every male in Israel, apart from Joshua and Caleb, who were from the previous generation, was circumcised. Flint knives flashed in the sun and blood flowed. Great was the agony and slow was the healing. Being an Israelite was not for the faint-hearted. Our God was a demanding God. They called this place, near Gilgal on the west bank of the Jordan – Gibeath Haaraloth – the Hill of Foreskins. Ishpah told us the tale and I wondered how high the hill was.

Another week dragged by and still only rumours. And another week, and another.

It was hard to carry on normally when at any moment an army of bloodthirsty Philistines might appear over the hill and come bearing down upon us. Eventually, I changed my resentful attitude and threw myself on God. I left the company of my ignorant and hot-headed nephews, Joab and Abishai, who were dragging me down to their own earthy and insensitive level – and gave all my attention to my family's well-being and the running of the farm. As I did so I communed with God and was encouraged in Him. I could feel the Spirit of God stabilising and balancing my own spirit and began to feel like one of those strange insects that walks and skates on water. By rights I should be sinking, but in fact I was borne up. This sensation infused my heart with hope. Each day seemed like a jewel: a gift from God. I spent some time with Ishpah. He said nothing much, which, for him, spoke volumes. He was contented with me. He approved.

In the sixth week of our vigil, my father could bear it no longer: "Go to the battle, my son. It has been too long! Something is amiss… Find out what is going on. The rumours persist: it is said that battle is still not joined – a great giant has filled our army with fear. A giant! – this surely cannot be… Load the donkey with these provisions for your brothers: wine, bread, raisins, fruit – and present this gift of cheese to the commander of their unit. Leave at first light tomorrow. And bring back some token from your brothers so that I can be assured of their safety. Do you know how to get there?"

"I do, father. The battlefield is in the Valley of Elah; I have been there with Sol. I know it well."

"Hasten back. Our whole village is on tenterhooks. The waiting is endless! Why is there no news? What can have happened? Come – I will bless you. May God grant you speed and protection and bring you home in safety – with good news."

I prepared the donkey, readied my travelling cloak and my military sandals – a gift from Saul – and set out at first light. I had my steel knife, my staff and shield, my shepherd's pouch, and a goats-hair sling made by the men of Gibeah. My previous sling of linen, Zeruiah's handiwork, was worn out; and it seemed frail and small by comparison. My goats-hair sling could fling further, harder and more accurately; and it was springy. I could swing it right-handed – but for extra power I would grasp my throwing wrist with my left hand and thus increase the torque and the revolutions. Below the steep walls of the palace at Gibeah there was a knoll, worn bare by sandalled feet. This is where the young wolves of Benjamin met to display their skill and prowess with the sling. A favourite (but frowned-upon) pastime was to hurl a large rock at the wall and watch it disintegrate – the rock, that is, not the wall – though the wall did suffer damage.

Watching the young men in action made me appreciate the value of a shield in warfare. Those rocks hit hard. In battle, the sling was mainly a long-range weapon, where distance and power, rather than accuracy, was required. A volley of rocks showering down on the enemy – especially an enemy in flight – was a useful tactic. But – there were also specialists. These marksmen were stationed at vantage points in a battle, if the terrain permitted, and their job was to aim at specific targets.

My journey to the scene of battle was accomplished by mid-morning and I came in from the east. This gave me a long-distance view of the valley of Elah. How I wished for the eyes of an eagle to help me decipher the scene before me. Not much was happening, it seemed. On one hillside the Philistines were camped, on the other was our army, standards fluttering. In between lay the broad valley, with the stream wriggling unconcernedly down its channel on its way to the ocean, which glinted in the distance. Dust blew lazily off the battle line. No immediate danger threatened. I wondered why this was so.

I reached the camp and left the donkey and the provisions with the supply officer. As I arrived our soldiers were taking up their battle positions, shouting the war cry in unison: "For Saul and for Israel!" How feeble did they sound, compared to the lusty response of our opponents! A thrill of indignation shivered through me. What sort of battle cry was *that*? – and what had been happening these last six weeks? Why was battle not joined? I pushed my way to the front and encountered my brothers.

"Greetings, my brothers! What is happening? Why is the battle still not joined?"

"You don't need to know," Eliab responded tersely.

Abinadab and Shammah glowered at me over his shoulder.

"What are you doing here anyway?"

"Why should I not be here?" I replied in surprise. "Father has sent me with provisions. He is eager to know the news. Everyone is waiting in suspense – what is happening?"

"You may well ask," Abinadab conceded: "Just wait. At any moment now, you may get the answer to your question."

Even as he spoke, trumpets sounded from across the valley. Trumpets and drums. Something was happening. Every eye in Israel stared across the plain towards the enemy. Our soldiers looked like frightened deer. I pinched myself. Was this a dream?

Two men came out of the enemy's ranks and stood in the dusty plain. One of them looked enormous. The other, his armour-bearer, was half his size. So – there *was* a giant! I studied him in detail. He filled my horizon. "Go home!" Eliab muttered at me bitterly. I hardly heard him. I continued to gaze at the giant. Never had I dreamt to see such a man! He was a colossus. Even though he was a bow shot away, every line and crease of his face stood out like crags on a hill: the broad, high forehead; the hooked nose; the massive lips framed by an ample beard; the large close-set eyes; the sneering look; the confident posture.

The Philistine champion halted well before the battle line and raised his spear in defiance. His massive features were contorted with pride and scorn. He was fully clad in battle gear. From head to toe. Bronze this, bronze that – leather jerkin studded with bronze: arm-guards, knee-guards, gauntlets, closed-in sandals. He wore a metal battle helmet that incorporated a chin guard, a neck-guard, and a full-face visor. He was impregnable. No wonder he stopped short of the stream: if he missed his step he wouldn't be able to get up. The helmet's visor was up, pointing to the sky, making him look like a behemoth with a shining crest. Our army was silent, like mice, transfixed by this dreadful apparition. Especially intimidated were the bigger, stronger warriors, and none more so than King Saul, whom I could see at a distance. His features were downcast, his posture failing. He was a man in the throes of fear and oppression. He was not himself.

"Give me a man!" roared the giant.

His voice was terrible, like rocks grinding. We had shared Canaan for two centuries with other nations and our languages had become intermingled. So, for the most part, we could understand him: his accents were strange, but the words were intelligible. "Give me a man!" he cried again, and his armour-bearer raised the mighty shield with an uncouth roar. They were a class act, these two.

The giant cursed us, long and loud; I looked around for someone to respond: all were silent.

"Why do you come out and line up for battle?" the man demanded: "If you do not dare to fight? Am I not a Philistine – and are you not servants of Saul? Choose a man! Choose a man – and have him come to me. If he is able to fight me and kill me, we will become your subjects; but if I overcome him and kill him – you will become our subjects: *you* will serve *us*. And you *will*! This day you will become our servants! I defy the ranks of Israel! Give me a man and let us fight each other. Where is the pride of Judah? Where is the man who dares to engage me in battle?"

Righteous fury surged up within me.

"Who is this uncircumcised Philistine, that he dares to defy the armies of the Living God?" I cried out to heaven.

My words cut through the tense and miserable silence of our army and heads turned in my direction.

"And what will be done for the man who removes this stain from Israel?" I demanded.

Nearby soldiers turned anxious faces towards me.

"He is the giant from Gath. Goliath…" one of them responded. "Morning and afternoon for the past forty days he has brought this challenge. Forty days! When will it end? No one dares face him. We can endure this no longer. The king will richly reward the man who can overcome him – with his daughter in marriage and freedom from taxes for…"

"You have no business here!" a familiar and impassioned voice broke in. It was Eliab, once again. He was glaring at me with a hatred that was fuelled by fear.

"I know what you're up to, you little sneak. Why are you not back in the desert with those few sheep? You have just come down to watch the battle, haven't you? Go back right now – because you have seen all that you are going to see. I will not put up with it! Stop your foolish talk and get out of here, before I give you what you need!"

"What am I doing wrong?" I demanded. "Am I not even allowed to speak?" I gazed briefly into Eliab's eyes and saw the fear that had taken hold of him. I shook my head, shrugged and moved on.

Where was the champion of Israel? Where was the man who would uphold the honour of the Armies of the Living God? Why not Jonathan, our great hero? Or Abner, our fearless leader? Or Saul, our king? Or Cush the Terrible. Or Eliab – my great big bossy brother?

While I was questioning some other soldiers, word reached Saul of this outspoken youth who was haranguing his troops and he sent for me. He seemed in another world: no trace of recognition came to his brooding eyes. I stood before him, youthful and unquenchable, in my rough shepherd's cloak and military sandals, my chestnut hair shining and blue eyes flashing. Suddenly, I found myself responding to this dread situation in a way I had never imagined. Words unprepared and unconsidered poured out of my mouth:

"Fear not, my father, I will destroy this boaster! How dare he defy the Armies of the Living God! Let no one lose heart on account of this Philistine: he will be meat and drink to me. Have rest in your spirit."

The gaze that met mine seemed to come from a dark and distant place. King Saul was before me in person but in spirit he was elsewhere. Behind him the awful Abner brooded, and next to him leant the youthful Jonathan, looking pale and quenched.

"You cannot fight him," the king muttered, looking at me strangely: "You are but a youth… and he has been a fighting man since his youth…"

"Your majesty," I responded, "I have been looking after my father's sheep for many harvests. On separate occasions, first a bear and then – a lion – came to attack the flock. I slew them both. I took the lamb from the mouth of the lion and when it turned upon me, I grasped it by the hair and struck and killed the beast. The Lord, who protected me from the lion and the bear, will give me victory over this uncircumcised Philistine. I will overcome him. The Lord who delivered me from the claws of the lion and the paw of the bear – He will deliver me from the hand of this Philistine. Fear not."

My words carried conviction. King Saul looked first to Abner and then to Jonathan. It had been forty days. Something had to be done. What other way was there? Abner looked at the ground. Jonathan nodded. The die was cast.

"Go, my son, and God go with you," King Saul agreed, but still as if in another world: "…but here, wear my armour for your protection…"

I gazed at him doubtfully. I was sixteen years old, and although sturdy and nimble had not yet reached full stature.

The king on the other hand, though old, was a huge man – powerfully built and a head taller than any man in Israel. And was he suggesting that I wear *his* armour for protection? Since I was half his size it was obvious that this was a bad idea. Nonetheless, I went through the motions of trying the armour on. Naturally, it didn't fit.

"This is no good," I announced decisively: "This will only hamper me. I cannot walk! Undo me; I will go as I am."

Rough hands fumbled at the loops and catches and released me. Lightly, I tripped down the hill.

Every eye was upon me. A whisper of horror fluttered through our ranks. I reached the brook in the centre of the valley and recognised the same crumbling bank I had once found on my journeys with Sol. A quick thrust with my staff and a piece of the overhanging crust collapsed and five rounded stones fell down and rolled into the shining water. I suppose they had been waiting for this moment since the beginning of creation. I fished them out and put them in my bag. Then I leapt lightly out of the channel and faced my adversary. A fierce, indomitable spirit gripped me. As I studied my opponent, I felt a relentless power surge through my being. My hand closed over the worn leather pouch where the five stones nestled, like eagle's eggs in a nest. I had five shots, and even if I missed them, I felt confident that I could tear my opponent limb from limb with my bare hands. I paused and stood – motionless and dramatic – for a timeless moment.

Goliath's face was a study. He was angry and offended. His visor was still pointing skyward, exposing his forehead, and he waved his armour bearer away and cursed me roundly by his gods. The Philistine host echoed his words and the valley filled with the thunder of cursing. I waited on the Lord, every fibre of my body thrilling with divine energy.

"Am I a dog?" the giant demanded: "…that you come at me with sticks? Come, little boy, and I will feed your flesh to the birds of the air and the beasts of the field."

"It is you who will die this day," I responded, vehemently, my voice ringing as I had never heard it ring before: "It is you who will be defeated. You come against me with sword and spear and javelin – but I come against you in the name of the Lord God Almighty, whom you have defied. This day He will hand you over to me and I will strike you to the ground and cut off your head. I will give your army to the birds of the air and the beasts of the field, and all will know that our God reigns. In vain do you trust in your own strength! All those gathered here will know that it is not by sword or by spear that the Lord saves – for the battle is the Lord's and He will give us the victory!"

Words tried to rise to Goliath's mouth, but he was strangled with rage. He held out his arms in mockery and half-turned towards his army, wobbling his head in derision. As he did so I fitted a stone to my sling, swung it with two hands, and on the third rotation let it go. I knew exactly where it was going. Goliath saw it just as it entered his skull. He collapsed on the ground and a collective gasp of horror and disbelief ran through the Philistines. A similar gasp, but of joy and disbelief, came from behind me. I ran forward, tugged the massive sword from the giant's scabbard, thrust him through and hewed the massive head from his shoulders.

The gasp of horror from his countrymen became a howl, and in that instant the hearts of my countrymen were restored. There was indeed a God in Israel. They raced down the hillside, no longer fearful and weak. They pursued and slaughtered the Philistines all the way to Gath and beyond. The Armies of the Living God were alive again.

*

I was led up the hill to King Saul, the giant's head still in my grasp. Abner accompanied me, dour and black. Jonathan was at the foot of the hill, refreshed and joyful, his visage a hymn of praise. King Saul stood motionless, completely confounded, unable to take it all in. I knelt before him and then arose, awaiting his pleasure. He reached out a massive hand and placed it, trembling, on my shoulder. He gazed at me with dark, troubled eyes in which a thousand nightmares were fading into oblivion, and spoke, in thick disconnected tones:

"Whose son are you, young man?"

"I am the son of your servant, Jesse of Bethlehem," I replied.

Chapter 20
The Chorus

"Beth - le - hem," he intoned: "Never has that name sounded so sweet. What do you think, Abner? Has not the Lord our God come to our rescue in a mighty way this day!"

"Indeed," Abner agreed, dryly. His battle-hardened features and grey-streaked beard glistened in the bright morning sun. His hawk-like eye glanced swiftly over me, then gazed west again. Dust rose in that direction. It was the dust of chariot wheels, and of a thousand pounding feet, as our victorious army pursued the fleeing Philistines to the gates of their distant cities.

"In… a moment of time… one's life… one's life is changed," the King said, in reverent tones. "I look to the hills. From whence does my help come? My help comes… from the Lord. Maker of heaven and earth. Let His Name be praised. My son…" he placed his massive hand on my head, "you are to be forever by my side. You are… to be forever… I do… I do remember you," he murmured: "… but sometimes the darkness creeps in and steals my mind. But now I see clearly. And it is the Lord's doing. You are God's gift to Israel my son, and from this time forth will be at my right hand."

Abner turned and looked me in the face. What did I see in that look? Love, gratitude, joy, respect? No. Rather – distrust, envy and resentment. It was the gaze of a man who has spent his life attaining to high position and who finds himself challenged by a nobody. For who was I? Does the slaying of one giant mean so very much?

But Abner was nothing if not perceptive. He could judge men, he could judge warfare, he could read the times and he could read men's hearts. For many years he had been Saul's right hand man. He was nearly forty years old, twenty years younger than his cousin the King. But as much as Saul was volatile and unstable, so Abner was steady and tenacious. His strength underpinned Saul. And… he didn't like me. That was plain!

I became conscious of a weight still clutched in my nerveless fingers, hanging at my side. Goliath's head.

A lone figure approached. The battle-field was deserted, the valley floor empty apart from the fallen giant. The camp of the Philistines on the opposite hill – was abandoned. For forty days they had occupied that hill, confident and scornful. Now they were fleeing back to their cities in terror. Pursued by our army. The lone figure threaded his way through our goats-hair tents and supply shelters, and approached us with a jaunty, boyish step. He bowed to the King, acknowledged the commander-in-chief, then turned dancing brown eyes upon me, the shepherd boy. He knelt before me, as one would before a hero or a king.

It was Jonathan, the crown prince, Saul's eldest son, ten years my senior and the hero of Israel – kneeling at my feet.

As Jonathan rose and placed his hands on my shoulders, Abner took the king's arm and led him gently away. The day seemed suddenly brighter. Jonathan kissed me on the forehead, as is customary between friends in our culture, and fixed me with sparkling eyes. All traces of the wan and fearful youth that I had witnessed so painfully only a few short moments ago, had disappeared.

Short moments may have lifelong consequences.

"How old are you, David son of Jesse?" Jonathan asked me.

"Sixteen," I responded.

He shook his head and gazed at me long and comfortably. Strangely, I felt no qualms of embarrassment or uneasiness. Quite the opposite. His gaze bathed my spirit in a cool and delightful freshness. Like a mountain stream running through a meadow.

"I love you… my brother," Jonathan stated simply. "I love you more than life itself. You are God's gift to Israel. Did not I hear my father say this very thing as I approached just now? Ah, but I have quick hearing and the breezes are kind. But let us enter into a covenant together before the Lord, you and I, to serve Him side by side, come what may, as brothers in His service."

He read the agreement in my eyes and falteringly, as if embarking on a new and undreamed-of adventure, I dropped my burden and drew Jonathan into my arms and kissed him in return. King Saul, who was standing some way off, witnessed this exchange and his countenance fell. My poor king, beset by fears and shadows on every side, his emotions and his spirit battered by every breath.

"Take my royal robe!" Jonathan commanded. "And my sword, my bow and my belt. And here, take my tunic as well. I will have yours. We are brothers in the Lord."

We exchanged garments and our souls were knit together as one. We embraced once more and as we stood there on that hillside, I felt a surge of irresistible power coursing through my body and my soul. It was the Breath of God, and we felt it together. We stood there, silent and transfixed, lifted up like eagles on the wind, while Saul and Abner stood scanning the horizon for signs of our returning army.

"What are you going to do with the weapons?" Jonathan asked eventually, nodding towards the giant's sword and shield at my feet.

"I will put them in my tent."

"And the head?"

"I don't know… What should I do?"

"Here they come!" Abner's voice grated. "Messengers – bringing good tidings – and the standards of your enemies, O King. Out of the way, boy!"

He shouldered me to one side and thrust his spear into Goliath's head, then in one savage motion up-ended the spear and thrust the butt end into the rocky ground, where it stood quivering and erect. "A fine standard of battle we have here, O King," he commented, gazing at the trophy, "and how your people will dance and sing your praises as we return in triumph."

"So why did you not overcome the giant yourself?" I wondered. Jonathan read my mind and looked into my eyes with a look that calmed my passions in an instant. I could see the Spirit of God looking out of his eyes. Calm, timeless, all powerful. I held my peace.

At last Saul spoke: "The army is returning. Let them plunder the Philistine camp and let us go. I am weary. I need to lie down, in my own bed, in my own home." He looked at me and I saw the turmoil of passions within him. My heart ached.

Abner brought the rams-horn trumpet to his lips and sounded a call to attention. Then, after a few seconds, he blew another signal. He was calling his commanders. The plunderers on the hillside resumed their scavenging whilst the commanders obeyed the call. I was standing next to Jonathan. As each man arrived, he knelt in salutation first before the brooding King and his fearsome General, then came to me and Jonathan and knelt before us in turn. But they had eyes only for me, these hardened warriors of a hundred skirmishes – eyes only for a youth half their age, with only one triumph in his tally. Yet clearly, that one triumph was worth ten thousand in their eyes. I was a hero: in overcoming the giant I had also won the hearts and minds of the men of Israel… with two notable exceptions, that is.

Abner consulted with his commanders. The king and three hundred picked warriors, along with Jonathan, Abner and myself, were to set forth immediately. The rest of the army was to follow the next day and meet the king at the training fields of Gibeah for dismissal. It was well into the ninth hour before we left: only four hours of daylight remained. Clearly, we would have to camp overnight. Gibeah, Saul's city, was a day and a half's travel away. Maybe we would reach Bethlehem before nightfall. King Saul rode on his mule. The rest of us marched and our spirits were high.

Our nation had no chariots or horses. Our enemies the Philistines did, because they lived on the level plains by the sea. We lived in the hills and the foothills where the gullies and valleys were unsuitable for chariots, especially in battle. It was fortunate for the Philistines that the track down which they fled was a good one, or the slaughter would have been greater. Once they gained their cities our troops fell back – to keep out of range of arrows shot from the high city walls. A few hot-heads strayed too close and paid the price.

After a battle the injured and the dead were brought home to their families, if possible. It was considered a disgrace not to be buried. However, for numerous reasons this was not always possible. Therefore, history was littered with battlefields where the dead on both sides were left to the elements and to the birds and the beasts. No wonder the eagle and the vulture and the jackal were abundant in our land. They haunted the fringes of the fray, knowing from long experience that whatever the outcome – they would have their share.

So, we set off, the king on his mule, in the mid-afternoon. As we left the valley, women came dancing out of the forest on either side of the track, with tambourines and lutes, to greet the conquering army. Word of our victory had gone ahead of us and spread like wildfire throughout the land. For many weeks the people had been on tenterhooks, constantly prepared to flee if the battle was lost. Now their joy and relief and exaltation knew no bounds. The women and children from the towns of Socoh and Azekah and from all the villages around lined our path as we zigzagged upwards through the low hills on our way back home. The mood of our militia was one of elation; shouts of joy and victory sprang to our lips. Wineskins, brought by old men from the neighbourhood, went from hand to hand. Trumpets and lutes piped and trilled and our unit fell into a marching step that sent us along like a wave, bearing all before us.

A chant, underpinned by Hebrew tambourines, began: a repetitive chant, ebbing and flowing like water.

"Saul has slain his thousands!" the women sang.

"Saul has slain his thousands!" echoed the marching men.

"Saul has slain his thousands!" sang the women.

"Saul has slain his thousands!" echoed the men.

On and on we went, the chant taken up by new admirers as the old ones fell away and returned to their homes. King Saul, on his mule, looked regal and serene; Abner at his side, strong and confident, holding high his spear with the massive trophy atop. As we reached the hills beyond Adullam a fresh group of welcomers renewed the chant. The army was silent now. Our march bore us on relentlessly. To our left, towards the distant glittering sea, sunset began shooting the skies with the blood of victory.

The revellers, many of them from Bethlehem, my home-town, took up the chant with a passion.

"Saul has slain his thousands," one group sang.

"And *David*, his tens of thousands!" a lone woman responded lustily, coming in early.

Who was that I wondered? Was it Zeruiah? In the half-light it was difficult to tell at a distance – but the woman was striking and dramatic, outlined against the western sky – and the voice… the voice was a bell.

A moment's silence cut the air, then the chorus resumed:

"Saul has slain his thousands!"

"And *David*, his tens of thousands!"

The echo came like thunder. Saul's shoulders slumped. His countenance fell…

I rued that chorus. It swept the nation, it was on every tongue.

"So begins the life-story of a mere shepherd boy with a heart after God. To be continued…"